"You're a cop. I feel it in my bones. I read it in every move you make.

"Who are you?" Ethan insisted. "And what are you doing here?"

"I think we've talked enough for one day," Michelle said softly.

"You can tell me. You can trust me. Maybe I can help."

"You can't help me. You have enough on your plate. Don't worry about me and what I have going on."

"I can't help it. I need to know."

"No, you don't. It's absolutely none of your business."

"If it's tied to this investigation—"

"I can assure you it's not."

"But there is something. Maybe we can help each other."

"You can help me by figuring out who actually did this. It was not Kayla Powers."

"Are you looking into something connected to the firm?"

"Good night, Ethan," she said abruptly. "I have nothing more t̶̶̶̶̶̶̶̶̶̶̶̶̶̶̶̶̶̶̶̶̶̶̶̶̶̶̶̶̶̶̶ ate it any more clear̶̶̶̶̶̶̶̶̶̶̶̶̶̶̶̶̶̶̶̶̶̶̶̶̶ ll me concerning my̶̶̶̶̶̶̶

D1462703

OZARKS DOUBLE HOMICIDE

MAGGIE WELLS

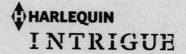
HARLEQUIN

INTRIGUE

For Sara, whose boundless enthusiasm and bottomless faith are
an inspiration to all who are lucky enough to have her on their
side. I'm so proud to be a part of Team Megibow!

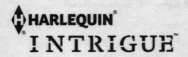

INTRIGUE™

ISBN-13: 978-1-335-58268-3

PLEASE RECYCLE

Recycling programs
for this product may
not exist in your area.

Ozarks Double Homicide

Harlequin Enterprises ULC
22 Adelaide St. West, 41st Floor
Toronto, Ontario M5H 4E3, Canada
www.Harlequin.com

Printed in U.S.A.

By day **Maggie Wells** is buried in spreadsheets. At night she pens tales of intrigue and people tangling up the sheets. She has a weakness for hot heroes and happy endings. She is the product of a charming rogue and a shameless flirt, and you only have to scratch the surface of this mild-mannered married lady to find a naughty streak a mile wide.

Books by Maggie Wells

Harlequin Intrigue

Arkansas Special Agents

Ozarks Missing Person
Ozarks Double Homicide

A Raising the Bar Brief

An Absence of Motive
For the Defense
Trial in the Backwoods

Foothills Field Search

Visit the Author Profile page at Harlequin.com.

CAST OF CHARACTERS

Michelle Fraser—An undercover FBI agent entrenched as a defense attorney at Powers, Powers & Walton. Trey Powers's former defense counsel, now representing Kayla Powers.

Ethan Scott—Lieutenant with the Arkansas State Police Criminal Investigation Division. Ethan is assigned by the division captain to take point in the investigation of a high-profile double homicide.

Kayla Powers—Tyrone Powers Jr.'s second wife and a former attorney at Powers, Powers & Walton. Now the prime suspect in the deaths of her husband and his son from a previous marriage.

Harold Dennis—The Powers family's personal attorney, and the biggest obstacle standing between the investigators and the truth.

Senator William Powers—Younger brother of Tyrone and uncle to his son. His campaign-fundraising group is the target of the FBI's investigation into a suspected Ponzi scheme.

Delray (Del) Powers—The senator's son. Generally believed to be the next in line to control the Powers family business ventures.

Chapter One

"Hey, Chief?"

Lieutenant Ethan Scott looked up to find one of his agents, Jim Thompson, hovering in the threshold of Ethan's office. It wasn't the greeting that made Ethan tear his gaze from the crime scene photos he was enlarging on his computer, but the hesitancy in the words. A big man, Thompson was usually full of bluff and bluster. But now, the blank expression on his face told Ethan his detective was shocked.

The guy had twenty years with the Arkansas State Police under his belt, and more than a dozen of them here with the Criminal Investigation Division. Shocking Agent Thompson wasn't an easy thing to do.

"What is it, Jim?"

"Powers." Thompson spoke the name softly. He stepped into the office, darting a glance over his shoulder as if checking to see if anyone in the office had heard him utter it.

Ethan nodded. He was too familiar with the name. The Powers family was all anyone around here had talked about for a month. Tyrone Powers Junior ran Powers, Powers & Walton, one of the most prestigious law firms in Northwest Arkansas. His brother, William, was a sitting US senator. And the son, Tyrone III—also known as Trey—was one of Company D's highest profile arrests in years.

"Grace is in Little Rock doing a depo on another case. Let Mr. Powers know she'll get back to them," Ethan responded tersely, then turned his attention back to the photo he'd been studying.

Special Agent Grace Reed had uncovered enough evidence to tie the Powers kid to the disappearance and subsequent death of a young woman named Mallory Murray, and since then, Grace, one of his best in the field, had been caught in the crossfire between prosecutors and the Powers family's formidable defense.

"No, that's what I'm trying to tell you, about Trey, uh…" Jim started again.

Ethan jerked his attention back to Thompson. "What about him? Please say he violated the terms of his bail."

Ethan was only half joking. He'd love to go snatch the smug jerk up and lock him away. With Powers behind bars, his legal team wouldn't be quite so keen on throwing every roadblock they could find in front of a trial date.

"He's dead," Thompson replied.

The bluntness of the answer left Ethan feeling as shell-shocked as Thompson appeared. "Crap." Swallowing hard, he raised a hand to rub his forehead. "Suicide?" he asked, eyes still downcast.

It was a logical assumption, considering the ever-growing list of charges pending against him, but Ethan had a hard time buying it. Guys like Trey Powers tended to be too egotistical to self-harm. They had all been operating under the assumption the arrogant young attorney had been raised to believe he was untouchable.

Above the law. But you never knew what went on beneath the surface in any person's life.

"No, sir. He was shot," Thompson corrected, jolting Ethan from his musing. "Both he and his father, um, Tyrone, were found dead this morning. I just got off the phone with the Benton County Sheriff's office. They're requesting our help."

Ethan shot to his feet. "Did you say both Trey and Tyrone Powers are dead?"

"Yes." Thompson nodded. "Sheriff Stenton said the wife came home and found them. Right there in the house."

Ethan gave his head a sharp shake, hoping to jostle the information Jim was giving him into some semblance of sense. "Are they thinking murder-suicide?"

Agent Thompson's indication of the negative came slow and deliberate. "No, sir. They say it looks to be a double homicide. Both were a single GSW."

The pronouncement made him drop back into his seat. Hard. Double homicide. The murder of a suspected murderer. And his father. A wealthy, prominent, politically well-connected man. The brother and nephew of a US senator.

This case would be beyond big.

There'd be a megawatt spotlight on this case until the killer was caught and brought to justice. It was the sort of investigation that transformed careers—for better or worse.

He was startled from his thoughts by the bleat of his desk phone. A glance at the display showed the caller to be Captain Will Hopkins, Ethan's boss.

Picking up the receiver, he said only, "Scott," by way of greeting.

The man on the other end didn't bother identifying himself. "Have you heard?"

Ethan blinked, wondering how his boss had gotten the news. But he didn't ask. Arkansas was not a heavily populated state, but the connections between its residents were as intricate as a spiderweb. Now that he'd had a minute, he wouldn't be surprised to learn the news had already made it to the governor's office in Little Rock.

"About the Powerses? Yes, sir."

"I want you on this personally," Captain Hopkins said in his usual brusque manner. "It's going to be a jurisdictional circus with the Bentonville police, the Benton County Sheriff's department and Lord knows who else besides us involved. I want you to run point."

"Yes, sir," Ethan responded, his gaze meeting Jim Thompson's for the first time since he picked up the phone. "I'm on it."

"Now," his boss stated.

Ethan rose from his chair, and Thompson's jaw dropped as Ethan started gathering his things. "Packing up now, sir. I'll need to run home and grab a bag—"

"Make it quick. I've dispatched forensics already. I don't want the locals getting too deep in the questioning though." He exhaled loudly, and Ethan could almost picture the man removing his glasses and rubbing at the bridge of his nose. "You know from the case with Trey Powers this is going to be a tricky one. The wife found the bodies. If I understand correctly, she's a lawyer herself, and by now she probably has half the lawyers at PP&W sitting on top of her."

"No doubt."

"You're my ace in the hole on this one," the captain asserted.

Ethan nodded. "I'm on my way. Check in with you once I get the lay of the land."

"Ten-four," Hopkins responded, then promptly hung up.

Ethan replaced the receiver, his mouth pulled into a grim line. Not many people in the Criminal Investigation Division were aware Ethan had a law degree as well. He didn't talk much about the six months he'd spent as a public defender, and how it drove him to pursue a career in criminal investigation, rather than defense. Watching people he knew to be guilty as sin get off on technicalities because the police were overworked and undertrained had been too frustrating to witness.

"He's sending you?"

Thompson hung back in the doorway, watching Ethan gather his computer, phone and cables, a look of surprise mixed with indignation heightening the older man's color.

"He is."

"You haven't been out on a case since you've been here."

Ethan's lips quirked, but he kept his head down, running through a mental list of all he'd need.

"True."

"Have you ever, uh—"

Thompson had the diplomacy of a battering ram, but at least had the good sense not to finish his question. And since he wasn't wrong about Ethan's lack of field time after joining Company D, Ethan let it slide.

"Don't worry, I caught some nasty cases down in Little Rock. I know what to do," he reassured the other man.

In truth, he couldn't wait to get at it. He'd been desk jockeying ever since Captain Hopkins recruited him for the job. Hopkins didn't care that he'd promoted Ethan over every agent already working as an investigator out of the Fort Smith offices. And, frankly, Ethan hadn't either. At the time.

He hadn't imagined how lonely it could be commanding a somewhat resentful crew in a town where he knew absolutely no one. He liked to think that in the past few months he'd cultivated some respect from the agents under him, but Thompson's incredulity was mildly insulting.

"It was bound to happen sometime," he said as he shoved everything into his computer bag. "I am an investigator, after all."

He gave Thompson a solid clap on the arm when he squeezed past the older man's bulk. As the senior agent in the company, Thompson would be in charge with Ethan out of the office. That should appease him somewhat. "I know you'll keep things running smoothly. I'll check in with you later once I talk to the captain."

Thompson gaped after him, his eyes darting to the desks where two other agents sat working, then to the empty desk Grace Reed usually occupied. "Do you want me to call Grace and tell her?"

Ethan didn't look back, nor did he slow his stride toward the door. He couldn't help feeling Thompson would take a little pleasure in telling the only female agent in the company that her biggest collar to date would not be facing justice after all. Not in a courtroom anyway. No, he'd make the call himself.

"I'll call her on my way," he said over his shoulder.

At the door, he stopped to look back at the open-plan office. All eyes were on him. And for the first time since he took over as their section chief, he felt no waves of hostility emanating from them.

Since he had their undivided attention, he gave one last direct order. "We're going to start getting media inquiries. I don't want there to be any comments coming out of this office at all. Refer all questions to the media liaison." He looked from one agent to the next. "Got it? No comments."

"Got it, Chief," Thompson replied, then gave him a sharp salute.

Ethan waited until he turned away to roll his eyes at the older man. He felt a sharp pang of remorse for what the other agents would likely have to endure under Thompson's command, but the man had seniority.

Sliding into the state-owned SUV that came as one of the perks of the promotion, he headed to his apartment to pack. Since he'd never fully settled into his place in Fort Smith, he figured it would take him less than thirty minutes to gather what he needed and hit the road. Still, given how quickly the news had traveled through the various law enforcement agencies, he figured he'd better get his call in to Grace Reed before taking the time.

He knew he was already too late when she picked up right away with a resigned greeting of, "Morning, Lieutenant."

Lieutenant. The use of his rank did not bode well for the conversation. Usually, she called him Chief. And until now, he and Grace got along well enough. They shared the uneasy camaraderie of being the two outsiders in the section.

"I take it you've already heard."

"About Trey Powers? Yes, sir."

"And his father, too," he added.

"Tyrone is…was," she corrected herself, "an interesting man."

Ethan didn't need to see her face to know the compliment was loaded with subtext. "I have no doubt." He drew a deep breath, then hurried on. "Obviously, we'll have to go through the formalities of dropping the charges against the younger Powers."

He heard her sharp intake of breath and winced. If he'd been in her shoes, he'd have felt the sting of it, too. "Yes, sir."

When she added nothing more, he figured he ought to let her have all the bad news in one fell swoop.

"I don't know if you've heard, but Captain Hopkins has assigned me to the double homicide."

There was a pause that lasted a breath too long. "I had not heard. Congratulations. This will be a big case."

"It will." For better or worse, he thought grimly. As he turned into the parking lot of his apartment complex, he felt the full weight of what he was about to tackle settle on his shoulders.

"Listen, I know you're feeling conflicted right now. We all are. You've put in a lot of legwork on the case against Trey, and I want to assure you that your efforts were not wasted."

"No, sir."

Her brief responses made it clear she understood those same efforts were unlikely to be rewarded in any way she deemed satisfactory. He'd been there before. There was nothing worse for a cop than to have a suspected murderer slip the charges, no matter how it happened. There would be no closure for either Agent Reed or the victim's family. Worst of all, no justice for the victim, Mallory Murray.

Pulling into his usual parking space, he killed the engine. "Listen, I have to pack and get up to Bentonville, but I want you to know I'd appreciate any help you can give me as far as background on the family," he continued.

"Of course," she answered succinctly.

He sighed again. "I know this whole situation is a bitter pill to swallow, but I have a feeling I'm going to need every resource I have at my disposal for this case."

"I'll do everything I can to help."

Her tone was still brusque, but a couple degrees warmer than it had been. He'd take it. "I'll be in touch. Probably a lot. You and the knowledge you've amassed in bringing those charges against Trey Powers are the greatest assets we have at the moment."

There was another prolonged pause, then, to his relief, Grace said, "I'll send my notes before I leave Little Rock. You'll have everything I know about the Powers family and the players at Powers, Powers & Walton before you hit Bentonville, Chief."

Chapter Two

Michelle Fraser sat back in the plush sofa cushions and looked around the exquisitely decorated sitting room. The home Tyrone Powers had purchased for his second wife did not disappoint. It was decorated with the sort of subtle sumptuousness only the very wealthy could afford. Plump cushions, thick rugs and rich window treatments. All in white.

Or sort-of white.

Michelle was no interior design guru, but she was savvy enough to be fairly sure not one swatch in the color palette used to decorate this elegant room had been tagged as *white*.

She imagined the throw pillow beside her to be called *parchment*. There were swirls in the plush throw rug beneath her feet that strayed dangerously close to *oatmeal*. And the watered-silk draperies that hung from ceiling to floor? The pearlescent sheer almost begged to be called *oyster*.

"Right, Michelle?" a husky voice implored, derailing her train of thought.

"I'm sorry?" she responded, jolted from her ruminations. "I was strategizing. What were you saying?"

Beside her, Tyrone Powers's wife—now widow—

sat in bloodstained workout gear, staring down at her hands. "I was only saying I submitted to them taking adhesives for gunshot residue first thing. I wouldn't do that if I had done it. My willingness to cooperate with the police has to count for something."

Michelle nodded and involuntarily looked down at the other woman's hands. She'd been allowed to wash them once she'd submitted to the field testing, but there were still streaks of dried blood in the creases of her knuckles. "Of course." Then she remembered the role she was supposed to be playing in this farce. "But you should have waited until I got here."

"I also let the sheriff know that I'm willing to hand over my clothing," the petite blonde seated on the sofa beside her said decisively.

Michelle gave herself a mental shake. She was supposed to be the one advising Kayla on these matters, not the other way around. But here she was, shell-shocked and wondering how the hell she ended up here, while the woman beside her sat preternaturally calm, cool and collected.

And covered in her husband's blood.

"Again, you should have waited until you had counsel present."

Kayla gave her a shadow of a smile. "Doesn't matter. I still would have submitted to the testing. Plus, I do know what I'm doing. I haven't forgotten everything I learned in How-to-Be-a-Lawyer School."

"Then we can assume you are aware no matter how cooperative you are, you're still their number one suspect until another candidate appears," Michelle said gravely.

"I didn't kill my husband," Kayla said without equivocation.

Kayla's singular focus on Tyrone was disturbing. "Your stepson was shot as well," Michelle reminded her tartly. "How about him?"

Kayla stiffened. "I'm not going to pretend Trey and I were best friends or anything, but no, I didn't kill him either. Which the forensics will prove."

Forensics were only going to work in her favor if evidence of someone else pulling the trigger became apparent. Presumably, traces of Kayla would be found all over the crime scene. After all, she did live here.

From the moment Harold Dennis, the family's attorney and one of the senior partners at PP&W, called from his vacation, Michelle had been trying to work out ways to keep the police from taking her client into custody.

"Tell me again where you were this weekend," Michelle prompted.

She wasn't exactly sure why she went with this particular question. Maybe it was because she was still wondering how the hell she'd gotten roped into defending this woman against possible double homicide charges. Plus, something about Kayla's answer sounded off to her.

Kayla gestured to the eggshell-pink yoga pants and matching hoodie she wore. "I told you, I was doing a wellness retreat."

Michelle's eyes narrowed as she studied her client minutely. She had no reason to believe Kayla was lying, but every fiber of her being was telling her she was. "At a spa? A resort? Was there anybody who can place you at this retreat?"

Kayla hesitated only a second before shaking her

head. "I was only trying to have a sort of meditation-yoga-self-care weekend," Kayla informed her. "The past few weeks have been...hectic, and I needed to get away by myself for a little while."

"Where did you go? What was the name of the spa?"

"Well—" Kayla gnawed on her lip for a moment "—I didn't actually go to a spa. I had the spa come to me."

"The spa came to you," Michelle repeated, keeping her tone deliberately level.

If she'd been questioning this witness on the stand, she would have gone in for the kill at this point. Kayla's story was riddled with holes. She only hoped none of those were bullet holes.

"Listen, I need you to level with me," Michelle said in her most no-nonsense tone. "You know how this goes. You know that any inconsistency in your story is going to result in you booking a room at the kind of place you never want to visit." She exhaled her frustration. "Come on, Kayla, you were in this job before I was. You know the spa story isn't going to hold water. You have to tell me the truth now."

"I was at our lake house. Alone." Kayla looked down at the hands clasped in her lap, but she didn't say anything more.

"You were at your lake house alone and..." Michelle prompted.

"Drunk," Kayla answered in a whisper.

The younger woman lifted her chin and hit Michelle with the most direct gaze she'd managed since their conversation began. "I was at our lake house alone getting drunk and staying as drunk as I possibly could."

The tingling at her nape eased. This was the truth at last.

"Why?" she asked directly.

The sheriff would be coming back any minute, and they needed to move beyond couching questions in niceties and social deference.

"Why not?" Kayla retorted. "I wanted to escape for a weekend."

Michelle looked around the expensively furnished living room in what was undoubtedly the nicest house in one of the city's most exclusive gated communities. What in the world made a person like Kayla Powers want to get away so badly? But that wasn't the question at hand.

"Okay, so you were at the lake house alone. Did anybody see you there? Any staff? Grocery delivery? Food delivery?"

Kayla shook her head.

"Did anyone local see you stop to pick up provisions? A grocery store clerk? Package store?"

"I brought wine from Ty's cellar," Kayla said, gesturing to the door. "I didn't eat much. Grabbed some snacks and stuff from the pantry, figuring anything else I might need would already be at the lake house." She wet her lips and a wry smile tugged at the corner of her mouth. "Turns out the corkscrew was right where I left it."

"Why were you trying to get away? Had you and Tyrone had a fight?"

Kayla shook her head. "No. Ty is Ty. Same as always." She tossed off the last with a careless shrug. "I mean, I'm not sure he noticed whether I was here or not, but that wouldn't be unusual. At least not these days."

"You two were having trouble?" Michelle prodded.

"Not trouble," Kayla said, a shade defensive. "Just… marriage." She heaved a sigh, then rolled her eyes. "I guess the new had worn off, you know? For both of us, really, but mostly for him. But Ty has always run hot and cold. He gets focused on things and can't see anything else. With all the stuff with Trey…" She trailed off and stared pensively at the Carrara marble fireplace. "I thought I was okay with things cooling down. Mostly, I was. The more disinterested he was, the more freedom I had," she said, her voice hardening.

Harold Dennis was going to have a conniption when he found out how far she was letting this go, but at the moment, she didn't have time to worry about the family lawyer's wishes. He'd better be hightailing it back to Arkansas if he wanted this handled any differently.

As it was, Michelle had somehow managed to get her part in this whole mess upgraded from defending a spoiled young man against possible reckless homicide charges to defending his stepmother in an undisputed double homicide case. And though she operated under the guise of being a criminal defense expert, she was actually an attorney who specialized in forensic accounting. An undercover federal agent who'd spent the past two years gaining the trust of Harold Dennis and the other big shots at Powers, Powers & Walton.

Before Michelle could formulate her next question, a sharp rap came on the door. It turned out to be more a warning than a request. Sheriff Stenton stepped into the room without waiting for a reply. A tall man with dark hair and a sharply squared-off jaw entered behind him. Unlike the sheriff, he wore plainclothes, but the aura of cop practically oozed from his pores. His bearing was straight, his shoulders almost as angular as his jawline and his eyes were alert and watchful.

Fighting the urge to place herself between this sharp-eyed man and her client was strong, but Michelle resisted. Shielding Kayla would only make them look at her even harder. Since Kayla had voluntarily submitted to the residue tests and fingerprinting, they were taking the full cooperation route.

"Mrs. Powers, Ms. Fraser, this is Lieutenant Ethan Scott from the state police Criminal Investigation Division out of Fort Smith," the sheriff said by way of introduction.

The sheriff's manner was slightly less deferential than he'd been before the lieutenant arrived, and that made Michelle uneasy. She eyed them warily as the sheriff settled himself into one of the plush armchairs situated adjacent to the sofa, where she sat beside Kayla.

"I'm sorry for your loss...losses," Ethan Scott amended as he gave them each a nod.

She waited for him to settle himself like the sheriff had, but Lieutenant Scott opted to stand. A subtle but effective power play. Michelle wanted to surge to her feet as well, but she wasn't willing to give him the satisfaction of believing them to be anything but open to the additional resources assigned to the case.

The sheriff's attitude remained cautious. She could work his hesitancy. With the lieutenant, however, she'd have to tread more carefully.

"Sheriff, as I'm sure you can understand, this has been very traumatic for my client." Michelle divided an even look between the two men before proceeding. "We are happy to cooperate with the investigation in any way, but I believe remaining here is causing Mrs. Powers distress."

As if on cue, Kayla began to wring her hands. "I never expected them to even be here when I came home today. They should be at the office," she said, turning and searching Michelle's face as if she might have any answers as to why the two dead men were not in their proper place.

"I understand, ma'am, and we do appreciate all of your help," the sheriff said with genuine sympathy. "But I'm hoping you won't mind answering a few more questions now that the lieutenant has arrived. We need to make sure we have a good grasp on the timeline."

Michelle sighed. They had already been over Kayla's departure from, and arrival back, at the house multiple times, but it wasn't like she could object to going over the basic information once again.

"Ask your questions, Sheriff," Michelle said quietly. "Then, can we agree this will be enough for today? Mrs. Powers is going to have her hands full as it is. She'll need to notify family and make arrangements."

They all knew the last part was pretense. By now the double murders had been all over the news, but still, one would be expected to place calls.

"Of course," Sheriff Stenton answered agreeably. "Now, you said that you left here early Saturday morning. About 7:00 a.m.?" he asked in a drawl as thick and slow as molasses.

"Yes, we've established that," Michelle responded for her client.

"Excuse me, but… Mrs. Powers?" The sheer command in Lieutenant Scott's tone drew all eyes to him. "I am sorry for your loss, ma'am, but I really would prefer to hear your version of events rather than ask questions." He darted a glance at Michelle, then returned the full force of those storm-cloud-gray eyes on Kayla. "If you wouldn't mind walking me through everything you did since leaving here Saturday morning."

Kayla twisted her hands in her lap again, but this time her fidgeting worried Michelle. She saw the lieutenant's gaze drop, too, and knew she needed to deflect attention away from her client's nervousness. Reaching over, she placed her hand atop Kayla's and gave what she hoped would appear to be nothing more than a reassuring squeeze.

"Tell them everything you can," she said gently, not daring to peek at the lieutenant as she spoke. "Once you're done, we'll turn your clothes over to the forensics team and get you out of here."

She could feel Lieutenant Scott's stare, but Michelle pretended not to notice. If he thought she was going to let her client stay here and be grilled while they carted the bodies of her husband and stepson from the house, or worse, be taken into custody after the questioning, he was going to have to come at her with some hard evidence of Kayla's involvement beyond discovering the bodies.

"I left here Saturday morning at about 7:00 a.m.," Kayla began cautiously. "I drove straight to the lake house."

"You didn't stop for gas or any groceries?" Stenton asked.

She shook her head. "I had everything I needed here or already at the house, so there was no need to stop," Kayla responded.

"And this lake house is on...Beaver Lake?" the lieutenant asked.

"No." Kayla shook her head. "No, it's the Powers family's place over on Table Rock Lake."

"And it's in Carroll County?" the sheriff prompted.

"Yes, sir," Kayla responded automatically.

Lieutenant Scott nodded as if digesting this bit of information. "Thank you for the clarification. Please go on."

"I was at the lake house alone most of Saturday and Sunday. I wanted to get away for a weekend. We've had a lot of social activities lately and it's been a bit of a whirlwind." She shrugged. "I did some yoga, watched some movies on Cineflix. Cooked. Drank some wine," she added, her voice slightly wobbly on the last word. "I packed things up this morning and came back. I thought I'd be coming home to an empty house. Ty's usually at the office early every morning, and Trey doesn't live here with us. I wouldn't have even gone into the family room if I hadn't heard the television."

"So you entered the family room and…" the lieutenant asked leadingly.

"I saw Trey first." Kayla closed her eyes. "He was slumped over the arm of the sofa. Then I saw Ty at the other end." She stopped and swallowed hard. "I mean, I saw his shoes," she corrected. She opened her eyes then and looked directly at the lieutenant. "He'd fallen over onto the cushion, but his legs were sticking out." She made a gesture indicating a diagonal angle.

"And then?" Lieutenant Scott prompted.

"I remember thinking how weird it was that they were watching NewsNet," Kayla said quietly. "Ty never watched NewsNet. He preferred to get his information from multiple media outlets, preferably print." She smiled sadly at that. "Lawyers. We like things in writing."

Michelle gave her a soft, understanding smile, but didn't chuckle at the joke. The two officers simply stared at her blankly.

"His brother's in politics, so he's supersensitive to spin. Wouldn't trust anything that didn't come straight from a wire service and hadn't been vetted by one or two or more sources. He thought television news was trash."

"What did you do then?" the lieutenant persisted.

Michelle bristled. Her client was giving everything that she had as far as her impressions of the crime scene. She didn't appreciate his pushing her into recalling the gorier aspects of the morning's events.

"I ran to Ty," Kayla said, looking down at her knotted hands again. "I ran over and shook him. I guess I must have. I ended up with his head in my lap and tried to make him talk to me. I was calling his name, and… oh my God, there was so much blood," she said in a whisper. "So much blood."

"You hadn't noticed the blood until that moment?" Lieutenant Scott asked, his tone dubious.

Michelle was about to object but Kayla simply shook her head. "No, not really. At least, it didn't register. I didn't really realize that Trey was dead, too, until I couldn't get Tyrone to respond to me."

"But you didn't touch your stepson's body?" the lieutenant asked.

Kayla looked up at him, her brow furrowing as if the answer should have been obvious. "What? No. I wouldn't…no. Ty was my husband. I could see Trey was dead, and I…we didn't have a close relationship." She gave her head a shake. "Why would I go to him first?"

"What kind of relationship did you have with Trey Powers?" Lieutenant Scott asked abruptly.

Kayla glanced over at Michelle, who jumped in.

"What relevance does her relationship with her stepson have, Lieutenant?" she asked stiffly.

"Her stepson happens to be dead as well," Ethan Scott responded as if explaining the most rudimentary facts to her.

"True, but Trey Powers was also a grown man at the time that Mr. and Mrs. Powers were married. She would not have had any kind of maternal connection with Trey."

Lieutenant Scott eyed Kayla speculatively, no doubt mentally calculating the age difference between Michelle's current client and the one that lay deceased in the other room.

"Trey Powers was almost three years older than my client," Michelle supplied. "She was closer in age to him than her husband."

"I see," Scott replied, making a note of the fact.

"If you've got all you need in terms of timeline," Michelle interjected, "I think it would be best if we get Mrs. Powers's clothing bagged and allow her to freshen up at this point."

"One more question," Lieutenant Scott cut in as they rose.

Michelle's chin went up and she answered for her client. "One more."

"Does your house have a security system that would monitor anyone coming or going either along the driveway or to the garage?"

Kayla blinked, then turned to Michelle, her face lighting with hope. "Yes. As a matter of fact, it does." She reached for her mobile phone and scrolled until she found the right application. "Here. This is the security system. You should be able to see me leaving here on Saturday morning and coming back this morning."

Michelle heard the note of triumph in her client's tone and hoped Kayla's confidence was born of the truth. If the security system corroborated her client's story, it would go a long way toward clearing her name.

She watched as Lieutenant Scott thumbed through the various camera angle views until he found one that satisfied him. "Okay, I see you leaving the garage Saturday morning. The time stamp says 7:09 a.m.," he told Sheriff Stenton.

"Sounds about right," Kayla said briskly. "And today I wouldn't have been home more than ten or fifteen minutes prior to making the 911 call."

Ethan Scott's brows furrowed as he stared down at the phone. "Sheriff, what time did the 911 call come through?"

Stenton looked down at his notes. "I show it came through at 10:46 a.m."

The lieutenant hummed, then made to hand the phone over, but rather than giving it back to Kayla, he gestured for Michelle to take it. "Unfortunately, it appears the home security system cameras went off-line sometime Saturday afternoon."

Chapter Three

The moment the door closed behind Ms. Fraser and her client, Ethan turned to Sheriff Stenton and asked, "How do you like the widow for it?"

Stenton shook his head. "It would be the simplest answer, but my gut is telling me no. I can't imagine being the second wife there'd be a lot for her financially. The first Mrs. Powers took Tyrone to the cleaners. Got a chunk of everything that wasn't held in the family trust."

Ethan nodded, digesting this information. "There are other motivators. It isn't always money."

"True. Only most of the time." The older man shook his head and gave a rueful smile. "Either way, I don't see this sort of crime being this particular lady's style. You know what I'm saying?"

Ethan thought it over for a moment and had to agree. "I don't feel it in my gut, either."

"She's been nothing but cooperative since the moment we arrived on scene. She's truly shaken, you can see there. And she's no fool. If she did this, she'd know she'd be the prime suspect. Wouldn't she want somebody else to discover the bodies and make the call? It would be easier to play the shocked and grieving widow without being covered in blood."

Ethan sent the county sheriff a sharp look. The man was far more astute than his good old boy demeanor let on. "Good point."

"Do you plan on taking her in for formal questioning?" Stenton asked, conceding the lead on this case without putting it in so many words. "I mean, you're welcome to use any of the offices available at the county building, if that's your inclination."

Ethan paced the immaculately appointed room, rolling the idea around in his mind. The sheriff was right. Mrs. Powers was cooperating, and with the help of her attorney, had offered them everything they could gain by taking her in, while at the same time blocking any opportunity they might have to question her further.

They would have her clothes, the residue tests and her fingerprints. Her lawyer would know that her client was a person of interest in this case and would hopefully keep her client from doing anything rash. There wasn't any reason to take her into custody for additional questioning other than for the optics, and Ethan couldn't see hauling a young and obviously shattered widow into the station coming across as a win on the nightly news.

He shook his head. "No, I don't think that will be necessary. As long as her attorney is open to her client being available to us as more questions arise, I think we'll be better off seeing what forensics can find here at the scene and looking into the security issue."

There was a tap on the door, and Michelle Fraser stuck her head into the small opening, almost like he'd conjured her.

"Gentlemen? May I?"

Ethan barely started to nod before she stepped into

the sitting room and closed the door behind her once again.

"Mrs. Powers's clothing has been bagged by Deputy Herrera," she informed Sheriff Stenton. "I agreed to the deputy staying close by while she showers and changes into clean clothes." She then shifted her icy-blue gaze to Ethan. "Will you need us to come in to make a statement beyond anything we've discussed here today?"

"No," he said. But it came out a shade too sharply.

He wasn't sure exactly why Ms. Fraser got his hackles up. She was acting in a professional manner. Still, he couldn't help thinking of Grace Reed's astute impression when asked about the defense attorney.

"She acts like an attorney, but she watched us do everything like a cop," Agent Reed had told him.

Caught in the laser beam of Ms. Fraser's unflinching gaze, Ethan could understand what his agent had meant. He'd dealt with dozens of lawyers over the years and hundreds of law enforcement personnel. If he were going to slot Michelle Fraser into one of the two fields based on his initial impression alone, the only thing that would nudge her into the attorney grouping would be the cost of the expensive suit she wore.

But her stance, her guarded expression and the way she scanned and read a room like the sweep of radar looking for a blip said *cop* to him as well. Of course, it wasn't unusual for persons formerly in law enforcement to attend law school and become attorneys. However, in his experience, they tended to gravitate toward prosecution rather than defense. They also lost some of a cop's watchful edge after a few years seated safely behind a desk.

Ms. Fraser appeared to be as sharp as a tack.

He'd seen her in the news footage covering Trey Powers's arrest and subsequent arraignment, of course, but hadn't registered more than she was the attorney for the opposition. She was far more arresting in person than she appeared on camera. Almost charismatic. He could see how Grace Reed had said the woman baffled her.

Ms. Fraser was a mass of contradictions wrapped up in a neat designer suit. Her hair was cut into one of those no-nonsense styles. A sleek cap that framed her heart-shaped face. Standard businesswoman hair. It shouldn't have been remarkable at all, but it was.

Most of it appeared to be colored a mahogany brown so deep it edged toward burgundy, but the bits surrounding her face—quarter-inch-wide sections pointing to her chin—were bleached nearly platinum blonde. He was no hairdresser, but he knew there was no way this color came from Mother Nature. Those streaks certainly were not put there by the sun. By all accounts, PP&W was a very conservative law firm. He couldn't help wondering if her hair color was a form of rebellion or misdirection.

"—the security firm."

Ethan shook himself from his observations in time to see her hand a slip of paper to the sheriff. "I'm sorry, what were you saying?"

She took a step back, then gave him a frank once-over as if trying to determine if he was up to going toe-to-toe with her. It was all Ethan could do to refrain from straightening his shoulders.

"I was saying, Lieutenant," she began in an exaggeratedly patient tone, "that my client has provided the name of the firm that handles the security for the Powers family lake house."

She cocked her head, and when she appeared to be satisfied that he'd heard her, she continued. "The lake house is held in the family's private trust, and as such only Tyrone and his brother William have access to request surveillance video from the property. Mrs. Powers has provided the contact information so that you may get in touch with someone at that company directly since neither her husband, his presumed heir or his brother are available at this time."

"Where is Senator Powers?" Ethan asked.

Ms. Fraser shrugged. "He's overseas. From what I'm told, he left last Friday night to meet up with a congressional junket heading for eastern Europe."

He was impressed and more than a little annoyed she was able to rattle off the man's presumed whereabouts so readily. After all, the senator was not her client. And there was that condescending tone again. If she and her client were being so transparent, why did she sound like she had a secret?

Her confidence nettled him. Maybe that was why he couldn't resist jabbing back.

"Impressive. Did he clear it with you personally before leaving?"

The attorney glared at him for a moment, then gave him a slow blink that told him he'd set himself up to be knocked back again.

"No, but his departure was well documented on the evening news. The Powers Family Foundation hosted their annual gala that night. The senator was only able to come for the cocktail hour before he had to catch his flight back to Washington, DC."

"Were you at this gala?"

The question popped out before he could vet it, but in the moment she hesitated before answering, he decided it was legit. After all, both deceased persons and his prime suspect were presumably there, too.

"I was."

"Was everyone at PP&W invited?"

She pursed her lips, obviously parsing the question for possible pitfalls before answering.

"I wasn't in charge of the guest list, but I would say it was likely everyone from the junior partners on up were invited."

"And that would be about…how many people?"

"From the firm? Well over a dozen. In attendance overall? I would guesstimate between two and three hundred."

"And all of the Powers family was there?" Ethan pushed.

Ms. Fraser met his gaze challengingly. "Everyone except Tyrone's former wife, Natalie."

Something in her tone implied she wanted to add a "so there" to the end of her sentence. And perhaps she should have. After all, she'd handed him an alternative suspect on a silver platter.

"Does the former Mrs. Powers live in the area?"

Sheriff Stenton shook his head. "Last I heard, she was in Little Rock."

"Do you believe that the former Mrs. Powers would have any reason to travel from Little Rock to Bentonville to harm her ex-husband?" he asked.

Ms. Fraser gave him an odd look. "Regardless of what her feelings for Tyrone may have been, Trey Powers was her son, Lieutenant."

The tips of Ethan's ears burned with chagrin. For a moment, he'd been so focused on the widow and the ex-wife of one victim, he'd completely forgotten the second. The man who—until he'd been shot—had been this woman's client as well.

But rather than backing off, he dug in. "What was Trey Powers's relationship with his mother like?"

Michelle Fraser actually rolled her eyes at that. "She doted on him. He was her everything. And the feeling was mutual."

"And his relationship with his stepmother?"

"Lieutenant, we've already established Mrs. Powers didn't have any form of maternal relationship with her husband's grown son. The two were cordial with one another."

"Cordial," he repeated, but she simply held his gaze and her tongue.

Ethan decided to switch tactics. "Back to the security system... If there's a similar setup at the lake house—and we'll have to see if there were the same technical difficulties there—I don't suppose you know if it's possible to get in touch with Senator Powers to get permission to access the footage?"

She shook her head. "I'm sure the family's personal attorney, Harold Dennis, will."

"And where is Mr. Dennis?" Ethan persisted.

"I'm hoping he's in a plane on his way back from Barbados. I'd be happy to let you know as soon as I've had word from him." She shifted her attention to the sheriff, then back to him. "My client has made arrangements to stay at a local hotel. I know you'll want her to be close by," she said flatly.

"Yes, we do."

"I'm surrendering her passport into your keeping as a gesture of good faith," she said, handing over the slim booklet.

There was an awkward silence. Her stance niggled at him. She looked prepared for anything—to charge in, dash out, throw herself over a body, whatever. It was odd. He could understand her wariness. She was, after all, an attorney, and therefore suspicious of anything anyone said. But the readiness Agent Reed had noted was also apparent. He made the mental note to look deeper into Michelle Fraser's background. Something about her didn't quite ring true.

When he didn't take the proffered passport, the sheriff gently removed it from her hand.

"We appreciate your client's cooperation, ma'am," Sheriff Stenton said, filling the conversational abyss. "You've been very helpful."

Stenton slid a glance in his direction, and Ethan forced himself to perform the necessary niceties. These were important people. Influential people. He'd been sent here to keep the investigation running smoothly. He needed to pocket his antagonism now; otherwise it might trip him up later.

"Yes, thank you, Ms. Fraser. And please give our condolences to Mrs. Powers again. The Criminal Investigation Division and all state police resources are at her disposal. We will catch whoever did this."

Her raised eyebrows told him that she heard the note of threat in his statement, but otherwise her demeanor remained cool and calm as she nodded to them both and said her good-byes.

Once the door was closed, Ethan turned his attention back to the sheriff. "I didn't have a chance to speak to the coroner yet. What's the ballpark on the time of death?"

"Based on lividity, he's guessing they've been gone over 24 hours," Sheriff Stenton replied. "We'll be able to nail that down once he gets them to the morgue."

"So we're looking at any time from Saturday morning to, let's say, Sunday noon," Ethan said as he contemplated the view beyond one of the floor-to-ceiling windows. "The houses are not very close together, but we're still not talking large amounts of acreage. The community is gated." He turned to look over his shoulder at Stenton. "Is the guardhouse staffed 24/7?"

The sheriff nodded. "They say it is."

"Is there also video surveillance on the vehicles entering and leaving at the gate?"

"I didn't think to ask that," the older man admitted. He scribbled something on his notepad. "I'll follow up."

"We know these gated places aren't as secure as people think they are. Could be delivery drivers in and out of here at all hours of the day and night. Most of the time they simply wave cars they recognize through." He crossed his arms over his chest and let his gaze fix on one of the mature trees they'd obviously worked around in building the home. "How old is this community?"

"Don't know exactly."

Behind him, Ethan heard the scratch of a pen on paper. "I assume that anyone that lives in this neighborhood probably runs in the same social circles as the Powerses?" The sheriff grunted, and Ethan turned to check on him. "No?"

"There are layers to the layers, if you know what I mean," Stenton responded.

"The Powers family would be in the top layer," Ethan ventured.

"Yes, but they don't always stay there. Even before William Powers was elected to the Senate, they were heavily involved in politics."

"You mean they mixed and mingled with the common folk, too," Ethan concluded.

"Yes. The gala thing they had Friday night would have been a mixed bag."

"How do you mean?"

"Most of the people who live around here probably were invited," he said, gesturing toward the window. "The top layer, let's say. But there would have been a lot of other people in attendance. People they'd know because it was to their advantage, but not necessarily friends you'd invite for dinner."

"Do you think that Mr. and Mrs. Powers were the kind of people who entertained at home?"

The sheriff shrugged. "There's a huge dining room table but could be for show. I'd think in his business he probably did have to entertain some. I know he fundraised for his brother's political campaigns."

Ethan nodded as he digested that. "So Tyrone Powers was a man of the people like his brother," he concluded with a sarcastic edge.

Stenton chuckled. "Not quite so down-to-earth as Senator Bill," he said, matching Ethan's jocular tone. "But he came down off the pedestal when he needed to."

"And his relationship with law enforcement?"

The sheriff closed his notebook and held his hands up in a helpless gesture. "Until this bit with the son happened, really not much of one at all. Their firm isn't the type to handle those 'If you've been injured in an accident...' cases."

"No billboards on highways?" Ethan asked.

"They barely have their name on the front door of the place." The sheriff got to his feet with an exhaled groan. "Lieutenant Scott, this is gonna be one hell of a mess. There's going to be a lot of tightrope walking, and I'm glad it's you and not me who has to toe that line."

"Good thing I stretched before coming," Ethan said, regarding the older man. "Are you sure I'm not stepping on your toes taking over like this?"

"Are you kidding me?" Stenton let out a mirthless laugh. "I'm up for reelection next year. I'd run out and buy a bow for this case if I thought I could get you to take it off my hands faster."

Ethan smiled at that. "I understand. I'll need some of your deputies on occasion and will definitely be looking to you for some insights, but don't worry—I don't mind making some people mad, if we need to. That's what I'm here for."

He clapped the sheriff on the shoulder, then nodded to the double doors. "Let's head back to the scene and see if anybody's come up with anything good. I wanna take another look before they roll the bodies out."

"You've got a strong stomach, Lieutenant Scott, I'll give you that," Sheriff Stenton said with grudging admiration.

"I don't know about that, but I got a strongly worded order from my commanding officer to make sure I get this thing sewn up tight," he said as the sheriff opened the door for them.

"I hope you've got a good hand with the needle,"

Stenton commented when they stepped back into the busy corridor.

Ethan watched the crime scene team move through the house. To any outsider it might look like chaos, but he knew every single person there had a purpose. As they made their way to the den at the back of the house, he tried to keep out of their way.

A thrill of purpose shot up his own spine. Some men hunted animals. Arkansas was a playground for people who wanted to catch deer, ducks and even bears and elk in their sites. But there was only one type of prey he was interested in. He liked to catch the people who preyed on other people.

The first thing Ethan noticed when they reentered the crime scene was the television. In all the hustle and bustle, no one had bothered to turn it off.

NewsNet broadcast in the background, the drone of the commentator filling the room as news of the gruesome scene they stood in the midst of scrolled across the bottom of the screen.

Reporters were following Senator Powers through an airport, cameras and microphones surrounding him as he walked with his head down and hand up to shield his face.

The headline in the crawl read: *Senator William Powers returning to Arkansas following the discovery of two family members gunned down in their own home.*

Ethan watched the bodies of those two family members being zipped into bags for transport, his mouth thinned into a line. On the screen, the senator's handlers shouted "no comment" as they attempted to flank the bereaved politician.

But before they cut away, Senator Powers looked up,

his gaze boring directly into the camera lens. The man looked haggard and more than a little annoyed.

"I do have a comment," he announced, speaking over the shouts of the reporters and his handlers alike. "I want to say here and now that my brother and nephew's killer will not get away with murder. The person who did this will be caught, and she will face justice."

Ethan and Sheriff Stenton exchanged a look. "I didn't mishear that, did I?" Ethan asked quietly. "He said 'she,' right?"

Beside him, Sheriff Stenton pulled out his notebook and scrawled another hasty note. "Yes, sir, he did. He most definitely said 'she,'" he responded grimly.

Ethan shot him a sidelong glance. "Put the passport someplace safe, Sheriff. And let's assign around-the-clock surveillance to Mrs. Powers's hotel." He turned back to the television, where the cameras followed the senator's progress through the doors to a Jetway. "We'll need to get in touch with the family attorney ASAP. Find out who benefits most from Tyrone's passing, particularly now that the son is out of the way, too."

Sheriff Stenton stiffened. "Pretty sure it's going to be one of the women, are you?"

"He said *she*," Ethan replied, his eyes still locked on the screen.

Stenton shook his head again. "I still don't see the wife doing this one, but when there's a bucketload of money involved, people never fail to surprise me."

"That's funny," Ethan replied grimly, turning to face the man beside him. "I'm never surprised what people will do for a bucketload of money."

Chapter Four

The hotel Kayla Powers retreated to was a medium-tier entry presented by a national chain. Still, it was the best the town had to offer. Though a half dozen major corporations called Northwest Arkansas home, five-star hotels were thin on the ground. Michelle took in the generic decor and her lips quirked. She assumed the sliding half door that separated the bed from the seating area was what qualified it to be called a suite.

Her client had changed into clean jeans and a long-sleeved top she continually pulled over her wrists and hands. The cop in her couldn't help wondering whether the gesture was born of a compulsion to hide her hands from view, but the woman in her knew better. Without asking, Michelle walked over to the thermostat and nudged the temperature up a couple of degrees. Her client was on the verge of shock. She wasn't having some kind of Poe-inspired reaction to the fact that she'd murdered her husband and stepson.

"They always keep these rooms so chilly," she said, her tone casual. Glancing over at Kayla, she asked, "Is there anything I can get you?"

"No. Thank you. I appreciate you being here," the other woman murmured.

Kayla sat perched on the edge of the couch, so Michelle dropped down into the chair opposite her. "Don't worry, Hal should be back shortly. I'm sure he booked the first flight out that he could get." Kayla told her she'd tried to reach Harold Dennis after calling Senator Powers, but had been unable to contact him.

"He's flying private," Kayla corrected.

"Excuse me?" Michelle asked, a frown creasing her brow.

"I believe he and Bill flew out on a private jet. A client's plane. Hal was going to drop Bill off in DC so he could make the junket, then head for the island."

Michelle resisted the urge to shake her head at the thought of somebody "dropping a person off" in their private jet. She'd been around these people long enough that she should have been accustomed to this level of excess.

"Oh. I hadn't realized."

But if Harold had taken a private jet to Barbados, he would be back in Arkansas as soon as possible, Michelle reassured herself.

"Either way, he'll be here soon, and he'll know how Tyrone would have wanted things done."

"I know how he wanted them done," Kayla affirmed, "and I don't think Harold is going to be much help."

There was an edge of weary bitterness in her client's words, but when their eyes met, Kayla's were clear and direct though red-rimmed from crying.

Michelle leaned in. Sometimes the best questions were the simplest ones. "What do you mean?"

"I mean that Ty and Harold were not always seeing eye to eye on things. Haven't for the past couple years.

Harold's a little more Bill's guy, if you catch my drift. I think he even stays in touch with Ty's ex."

"Trey's mother?" Michelle asked, buying a little time to slot bits of information into place. She wasn't entirely sure that she was picking up all the nuances of the dynamic between the two Powers brothers, but she got the gist of her role here.

Harold Dennis wasn't going to swoop in and rescue her from babysitting Ty Powers's widow. Not if Kayla had anything to say about it.

"Yes. His mother, Natalie."

"I see," she said noncommittally, leaving the door open for Kayla to expound. She needed more data, but like everyone else, she'd forgotten that the woman seated across from her was more than a trophy wife. "Yes, I've met her."

"Right. Because of Trey."

"Because of Trey," Michelle confirmed.

"I've been thinking... I'd like you to stay on as my personal attorney," Kayla stated bluntly.

"I'm not sure how Harold—"

"Harold might resist, but I get to say who my attorney is, and I want that to be you."

Michelle closed her eyes for a moment, absorbing the implications of what Kayla was asking her to do. Not only would she be defying the man who she assumed would be taking over the reins at PP&W, but also, if she did so, she'd be taking prime time away from the mission she had hoped to complete this week.

She was supposed to be punching her ticket out of Arkansas, not getting herself even more entrenched in the mysteries and messes the Powers family managed to make of their lives.

"Tyrone and I drew up new wills," Kayla said quietly. Michelle looked over to see the younger woman twisting her fingers into knots, her head bowed.

"New wills?" she prompted.

"His previous will designated Natalie, Trey's mother, as Ty's secondary beneficiary," Kayla explained. "After we were married, he wanted to change it."

"Naturally," Michelle said encouragingly.

"But Harold always put it off."

"Because Tyrone wanted to put you in his will?"

"Trey was still his primary beneficiary," Kayla said a shade too quickly. "But there were also some changes on how he wanted to handle the business of the firm."

Michelle slid to the edge of her seat. "Changes that will impact...?" She left the last part of her question dangling, making it clear she expected her client to fill in the blanks for her.

"In the previous iteration, Harold Dennis or Del would step in to act as managing partner in the event of Ty's death. At least until Trey was ready to take over the reins."

"Del? Senator Powers's son?" Michelle frowned. Delray Powers hadn't struck her as much of a force in the firm. As a matter of fact, she often forgot the quiet tax attorney was actually part of the same family as the more dynamic Powers men. "Are you saying Delray Powers would be in charge?"

"If Tyrone died, Hal would manage the transition until Trey was ready to take over. If Trey were to die, then Del would take over as managing partner until the next generation could step in. That is, unless Senator Powers saw fit to give up his political career and come back to the practice of law."

"And in this new will?"

"Well, it's not going to make me look very good," Kayla admitted, meeting Michelle's gaze. Her lips twisted into a self-deprecating smile. "The new will designates me as the managing partner of Powers, Powers & Walton." She drew a deep, shuddering breath. "In perpetuity, unless Senator Powers opts to come back to the firm."

Michelle slumped deeper into the chair. "I see." She paused for a moment. "When were the new wills drawn up?"

"Over a year ago."

"Right. Okay," Michelle said, nodding as she digested the information. "But why then?" she asked, knowing it would be the first question the police asked once they found out about the changes made to favor the widow. "You've been married longer than a year."

"Like I said, Harold put him off and I think they both forgot. Then, Ty had an episode," Kayla said, her voice quavering though her gaze remained direct. "His heart. He thought it was a heart attack, but turned out to be angina. It was enough of a scare to spur him into rethinking his affairs."

"I see."

"It all comes to me," she said.

Michelle stared hard at the other woman, trying to detect even a glimmer of triumph or pride in the simple statement, but she saw none. Her client was stating facts. Facts that were not going to reflect favorably on her once the police were made aware of them.

"Okay," Michelle said quietly, her mind reeling as she sorted through the various options on how to approach this newest dilemma.

"I think we should get out in front of it," Kayla said with careful deliberation.

Michelle's thoughts were trailing along the same lines, but she was curious about her client's willingness to continue laying all of her cards out on the table. "What exactly do you mean by 'get out in front of it'?"

"We need to tell the police about the will before it's read and enters probate. I want them to know I'm aware that it won't reflect well on me and that I am continuing to cooperate as best I can."

"Who else knows about the will?" Michelle asked, her eyes narrowing.

"Only the people we asked to witness and notarize it," her client replied quietly.

"People who I assume have no connection to PP&W?" Michelle asked bluntly.

Kayla nodded. "We used a friend of mine from law school to draw up the papers. She works for a firm in Little Rock," she said. "Anderson & Associates. Two of the partners witnessed our signatures." She looked up. "Tyrone was wary of how interconnected everybody is up here. He specifically wanted an outside firm with no ties to either the Powers family or the Waltons."

"Difficult to find in this state," Michelle commented.

"True," Kayla said with a short, sharp laugh. "My friend graduated from University of Arkansas Law, but she's from Oklahoma originally and did her undergrad there. The partners in the firm where she works are both graduates of the U of A at Little Rock."

"I see. Not the caliber of institution that fits the PP&W recruiting profile," Michelle concluded.

"Exactly. Tyrone was well aware of the network in which he operated. He also was cognizant of all the treachery inside it. He was fairly certain Harold was trying to push him out at the firm."

"Push him out? Could he do that? I mean, Tyrone is a name partner. He inherited the lion's share in the firm, didn't he?"

"Push him out as managing partner, I mean," Kayla clarified. "Harold was convinced that he could run the place better than Ty could. And though he'd never say so out loud, I think Bill resented the amount of sway Ty's position gave him in the area."

"The amount of sway?" Michelle repeated, incredulous. "He's a sitting US senator. Who would have more sway?"

"Ty had more say in the day-to-day running of the family business. As the elder, he not only inherited the name, but he was also given controlling interest in the firm. That's no small thing. Everyone who is anyone up here uses our firm."

"How much of an ownership differential are we talking?"

Kayla shrugged. "Our prenup only addressed what I could expect from the portion of the family trust Tyrone controls. I've never seen the details on it, but I know that Bill was far more financially dependent on Ty than he wanted to be. Maybe a 60-40 split?" she hazarded.

"Wouldn't that still leave Bill a very wealthy man?"

"I know his divorce from his first wife cost him quite a bit," Kayla said softly. "He never stops complaining about it even though they've been divorced for nearly twenty years."

"Didn't your own husband's first wife take a good bite out of his net worth?" Michelle asked, hoping the blunt question would startle more truth out of her client.

"Definitely. But he had more to start with, so it didn't hurt as much. Plus, Tyrone was actively generating income for the firm. Bill and Anthony Walton had to step back in order to fulfill their new positions as senator and Judge. Bill is reliant on his salary as a public official and had to report his income from the firm in accordance with congressional guidelines, which limits income earned outside of his public salary. Needless to say, his public income did not allow for the lifestyle he was accustomed to living in, so Ty covered a lot of his personal expenses."

"And he always has to be out fundraising." Michelle considered. "Not only did he have to ask his brother for funds to live, but he has to ask the public for funds to run."

"Exactly," Kayla confirmed. "And he's not nearly as gracious about the personal contributions as the public ones."

Determined to get the conversation back on track, Michelle leaned forward again. "Harold doesn't know about the new will either," she concluded.

Kayla shook her head. "There's a copy in our safe at the house, one in Ty's office safe and one on file with the firm who helped us execute them."

"Who has access to those safes?"

"I have access to the safe at home. I'm not sure about the office. It's possible Trey had access to both of them," Kayla conceded. "I'm fairly certain Bill did not. And like I said, Ty didn't trust Harold entirely."

"So, I'm assuming you want me to approach the police with this information about the revised wills before it would naturally come to light," she said, raising an inquiring eyebrow.

Kayla nodded. "It's like with what happened at the house. I have nothing to hide. We have our reasons for drawing up the documents we did, and it was done quite a long time ago."

"You are aware that gunshot residue can't prove anything conclusively, and most law enforcement agencies in this state don't even ask for it, aren't you?"

"It can prove that I have not been anywhere near anything that discharges gunpowder," Kayla reasoned. "Offering the samples can't hurt me. I did nothing wrong, though I'm sure there are some people who have already tried and convicted me."

"What makes you say so?"

When their gazes connected again, Kayla's eyes were clear and direct. A blue so pale it was almost translucent.

"I know what people think about me," she said flatly. "I know what my old friends at the firm say, and I know what the biddies in society say. I know what everyone says. They think I set my sights on Tyrone because of who he was and what he had, but I loved my husband, Michelle." Clasping her hands together, she gave a helpless little shrug. "People can believe it or not, but I really did love him. And he loved me. We were a good match, and we were happy. Happier than some people could stand."

The last sentence took Michelle by surprise. "What do you mean by that?"

Kayla sighed. "Not everybody was happy to see Tyrone so content with his life. Even people who should have been."

Michelle heard the resentment ringing through each word the woman spoke. She'd spent enough time in Trey

Powers's company to understand exactly how entitled the young man was. "You mean Trey."

Kayla inclined her head slightly. "Yes."

"I thought you said you two got along. He told me that you did."

"I thought we did." The words came out in a voice thick with pent-up emotion. "I guess that makes me more foolish than I ever thought I was."

Michelle watched as the younger woman dashed a tear from the corner of her eye. "You think Trey was only feigning his friendship with you?"

It wasn't a stretch. Trey Powers was one of those guys who used the people and things that were placed in his path, then forgot about them the moment they were depleted.

"I suppose you ought to tell the police this as well," Kayla said, swallowing down the emotion that made her voice tremble. "Trey said some fairly ugly things to me at the gala Friday night."

"What sort of ugly things?"

"Oh, the usual stuff. Gold digger. Sleeping my way to the top. Some hateful comment about how he'd have to get Harold to double-check and see if I actually was a member of the Arkansas bar or if I faked my way into the firm to get to his father."

"He said all this without provocation?" Michelle probed, knowing that it wouldn't be unusual for the young man to do so without reason, but she had to ask.

"No provocation from me," Kayla said, stiffening her spine. "People were talking about him, though. Gossiping about the charges pending against him and debating whether they thought he was guilty or innocent." She snorted. "How can anyone ever apply the word *in-*

nocent to Trey Powers in any context? The man was born a piece of work."

"People at the gala were talking about him, and he lashed out at you because—" Michelle prompted.

Kayla threw her hands up. "Deflection? I don't know." She shook her head hard. "People love to talk about me, so maybe he thought if he turned the focus in my direction, they'd stop looking at him so hard. Either way, I told him I didn't appreciate being the family punching bag."

"And what did he say to that?"

Michelle didn't have any difficulty conjuring up the numerous ugly things Trey Powers could have trotted out. As handsome and cool as the young man was on the outside, on the inside he was seething with molten hot vitriol. He resented everyone and everything that ever stood in his way of getting exactly what he wanted in life.

"He made some comment about how I wouldn't have to worry about being a member of his family much longer, if things kept going the way they were going." The desolate expression in Kayla's eyes made it clear Trey's words had struck home with her.

"He believed you and his father were having difficulties?"

Kayla shrugged. "I don't know how, but I suppose so. The worst part was that he said it loud enough for everybody around us to hear." She gave a bitter laugh. "All of a sudden, they were no longer talking about the charges pending against Trey. Mission accomplished, I guess. By the time we left that night, everybody was eyeballing me as if it was the last time they'd have to see me in one of their ballrooms."

"Did you speak to Tyrone about it?"

"I tried to on the way home," Kayla confessed.

"What did he say?"

"He dismissed it all. Said there was nothing wrong with us. That we were settling into a normal marriage, and people love to gossip. He was upset with Trey," she said, adding a pointed look for emphasis. "He didn't appreciate his own son using him to deflect, I guess."

"How did you and Tyrone leave it?"

"We simply…left it." Kayla opened her hands in a helpless gesture of futility. "We went home, we got ready for bed, he kissed me good-night and within minutes he was snoring."

"And you?"

Kayla flashed a self-deprecating smile. "I went down and finished off the bottle of Chardonnay I'd left in the fridge after lunch."

"Had you had much to drink at the party?" Michelle persisted.

Kayla shook her head. "Not nearly enough. Ty didn't like me drinking in public. Apparently, Natalie had a tendency to get a little too far into her cups and run her mouth at social functions. It was one of the things he told me from the start would be a deal-breaker."

"And the drinking thing…" Michelle asked leadingly.

"As far as I know, Ty wasn't aware. Or didn't care as long as I didn't do something to embarrass him."

"But you were upset after the party," Michelle stated simply.

"Well, sure I was. I mean, I'm not supposed to embarrass him, but it doesn't matter if his son humiliates me? I was angry."

"So you took off the following morning to punish him?" she hazarded.

"Partially." Kayla huffed. "I guess it was more like I wanted to see if he'd even notice I was gone."

"Did he?"

"I got a text Saturday evening. After he realized he hadn't seen me all day long. He'd had a round of golf scheduled and was up and out early. And truthfully, it wasn't too unusual for us to go a whole day without seeing each other. I guess I should be happy he did notice eventually."

"What did you tell him?"

"I said I was tired and needed to get away, so I went to the lake house."

"And he had no problem with that? He didn't want to join you there?"

Kayla winced. "Truthfully? I think he was a bit relieved. Ty is…was drama avoidant. I'm assuming he invited Trey over so he could lecture him on proper family decorum in public settings, yada yada."

"Was Tyrone the type to lecture?" Michelle pressed.

The corner of Kayla's mouth kicked up. The stare she leveled on Michelle spoke volumes. "We're all attorneys. Lecturing is what we do."

"Good point."

"Listen, I know what the optics are here. I'm the second wife, the social-climber-turned-closet-drinker who stands to end up with a lot more than most people would think I'm entitled to," she said.

Her delivery smacked of the calm and measured cadence used in closing arguments, and Michelle was growing too aware of Kayla's background in criminal defense. Feeling a need to pace, Michelle rose, rubbing her palms together as she tried to gather her thoughts.

"I realize it goes against the grain to give up information to the police right off the bat, but I'm telling you, I have nothing to fear here. I did not do this," Kayla assured her.

Michelle sighed and stopped pacing. "I believe you didn't kill them, but I am not on board with the 'nothing to fear' part," she said frankly. "What if someone is trying to set it up so you *do* look guilty? What if there's enough circumstantial evidence for them to put together a cohesive case for a grand jury? It's what happened with Trey in the Mallory Murray case. They piled those circumstantial bits up until they were a mountain too big for anyone to ignore."

Kayla nodded. "I understand. But there are two big differences between me and Trey."

"What are those?"

She held up one finger. "One, I didn't do it." She added a second finger to form a victory sign. "Two, I am not going to even attempt to hide anything from the authorities. As far as I'm concerned, they have full access to every facet of my life."

Michelle pursed her lips and dropped back into the seat across from her client. "Even the personal stuff? Your worries about your marriage? The drinking?"

"Full access."

Nodding, Michelle digested her client's plan for mounting her defense. It was as good a plan as any. Trying to hide evidence and avoid questioning by the police sure hadn't done Trey Powers any favors. "I suppose you want me to pay Lieutenant Scott a visit and convey your intention to continue to cooperate fully?"

Kayla nodded. "Yes. And you have my explicit permission to share the personal, private information I have given you, if you think it will help them move past me as a suspect. I realize as the spouse, they have to give me a good, hard look, but I also don't want them to let the trail grow too cold while they do."

"Noted." Michelle stood and grabbed her bag. She gave the generic hotel suite one last appraising sweep. "Do you want me to bring you dinner—"

She turned back to find her client had curled up in a ball on the end of the sofa, a throw pillow clutched to her chest. Gone was the clear-eyed attorney who wanted to make certain the investigation was steered in the right direction. In her place was a young, vulnerable widow who appeared to be alone in the world.

"I'm okay," Kayla insisted, even though it was clear she was not.

"Is there anyone I can call for you? A friend? Your parents?"

Kayla shook her head. "My parents are on a cruise. I've spoken to them, and we checked flights from their next port of call, but it would take them the better part of two days and four flights. They're scheduled to be back in port in three days, and since we can't hold any kind of funeral or memorial until the coroner releases the bodies, I told them not to rush back."

Michelle twisted the strap of her bag around her hand, feeling torn about leaving Kayla to her own devices after such a traumatic day. But they weren't friends, and a friend was what Kayla needed at that moment, not an attorney.

"How about a friend? Is there someone who might come stay with you?"

Kayla's lips twisted into a sad smile. "I've been moving in Ty's world the past few years, and even before that, I mostly hung out with other attorneys from PP&W. Most of my school friends have gone to Little Rock or elsewhere. And the people up here…" She drew a shaky breath, then let it go. "I'm not sure I have any I can call my own."

Sympathy tugged at Michelle's gut, but she tamped it down. She and Kayla were not friends, and to even attempt to step in as one now would be disingenuous. "Okay, well, you have my number if you need anything."

"I do. Thank you."

Michelle passed the overpriced mini bar as she headed for the door. Gripping the handle, she turned back. "I hate to say this at such a time, but it really would be best if you tried to keep a clear head for the next few days."

Kayla didn't even turn to look at her. "You mean you want me sober," she said baldly. "I don't know that I can promise that."

Biting her lip, Michelle shifted into negotiation mode. "Can you keep it to the room? I mean, it might not look too good if anyone were to spot you hanging out at the hotel bar."

She heard the other woman's harsh chuckle, but Kayla still didn't turn to look at her. "Sure. Absolutely."

The affirmation was quiet but firm. As Michelle opened the door and stepped into the corridor, she heard her client say, "I've gotten really good at drinking alone."

Chapter Five

Ethan sat back in the squeaking chair he'd requisitioned from a desk the clerk told him was currently unoccupied. The office he'd been offered at the Benton County Correctional Complex was not much bigger than a broom closet, but at least it had a door. He hated trying to work in a warren of open cubicles.

His laptop sat open on the desk, but it was his phone that kept drawing his attention. He hadn't expected a phone call from Michelle Fraser first thing in the morning. Frankly, hearing her voice on the other end of the call had freaked him out. He couldn't help wondering if she had somehow sensed he'd spent a good portion of the previous evening digging into her background info.

The information he'd found showed her to be nothing more than what she claimed to be—a highly qualified attorney working for the area's most prestigious law firm. She'd done her undergraduate work at Boston College and graduated from Harvard Law. After graduation, she'd worked as an associate in a boutique law firm in Boston, then a midmajor in Philadelphia, before making quite a name for herself in corporate defense at a large firm in New York.

The partner track at a firm the size of Colins and

Preston was arduous and fiercely competitive. Maybe it made sense for her to jump ship and move to Northwest Arkansas when PP&W came calling. She'd come in as a junior partner, a fact that had to tick off at least some of the more senior associates. But none of that explained why she made his cop radar ping.

He sighed and pulled up the document where he'd added a page of facts the defense attorney supplied to the Powers case notes. She'd been as cooperative as her client, informing them of Kayla Powers's hotel information as soon as she'd seen the shaken widow settled. She'd answered the few questions he'd wanted to clarify from his notes without hesitation or any sign of dissembling.

It wasn't until she'd requested to meet with him in person to give some of her own thoughts on the investigation that he remembered she knew both of the victims well. She'd confirmed Trey had been her primary client in the months since his arrest in connection to Mallory Murray's death. And as a junior partner and the lawyer defending his only son and heir, she'd had extensive interaction with Tyrone as well, Ethan imagined.

Though he was convinced there was more to Michelle Fraser than met the eye, Ethan still didn't like the widow Powers for the double homicide. But he couldn't base an investigation on gut instinct. Until more evidence came to light, Kayla Powers had to remain their primary suspect.

He rocked back in his chair, laced his fingers behind his head and stretched his chin toward the ceiling, hoping to ease some of the tension in his shoulders before Ms. Fraser arrived.

But it wasn't meant to be.

A sharp rap on his door startled him from the stretch. His arms fell to his side and he jerked upright in his chair. The woman standing in his doorway smiled one of those closed-lip, "caught ya" kind of smiles. He was struck anew by how unlike his vision of a corporate attorney she was. Sure, she wore a suit, but this one was a sky-blue color that made her eyes pop. A plain white blouse dipped low enough to give a tantalizing peek of clavicle, but nothing so revealing as cleavage. The chunky blonde streaks that framed her heart-shaped face came to a point at her chin. She wore tasteful jewelry and low-heeled pumps and carried an expensive-looking leather satchel he assumed doubled as briefcase and handbag. "Oh. I didn't expect you to get here so quickly," he said, trying to play it cool as he lowered the lid of his laptop.

"I'm sorry. I didn't mean to startle you. I live on this end of town so I was nearby. I know it's early, but I imagine it's going to be fairly chaotic at the office today, and I wanted to be sure I spoke to you before I got caught up in it."

He turned to the chair across from the desk. "Please, take a seat."

She settled into the hard wooden guest chair that had been in the office when he took it over. He watched her every movement carefully, trying to get a better read on the woman. But she gave little away. She set her bag on the floor at her feet, then sat back. She held no note pad and carried no phone or laptop, though he was sure both were in the bag. Instead, she folded her hands neatly in her lap, the small smile firmly in place as she met his gaze directly.

He wished he didn't find her calm competence so

intriguing. She and her client were doing everything they could to make his job easier. He simply didn't understand why.

"My client asked that I come here to speak to you directly about some of the circumstances around the business of PP&W. There are some incidents that may come to light in the coming days."

"Incidents?" He sat up straighter, automatically reaching for a pen and the notepad. He preferred to keep things analog when having a conversation. He found people were more forthcoming when he had a pen in hand and his eyes on them, rather than his head down typing. Plus, maintaining eye contact allowed him to get a better read on the person delivering the information. "What sort of incidents?"

Ms. Fraser sighed, and he surmised she was feeling torn about her client's strategy of full cooperation. He couldn't blame her. People often acted against their own best interests. As a lawyer, he'd seen more than his share of defendants insist on taking the witness stand against counsel's advice and common wisdom, but it was difficult to convince someone that they might not be the best narrator of their own story.

"I'm told Mrs. Powers and Trey had a bit of a run-in at the Powers Family Foundation gala the night before she left for the lake house."

"Told by Mrs. Powers?" he prompted, wanting the clarification.

"Yes."

"What kind of run-in?"

She sighed again, and the attorney in him felt for her, even as his cop fingers clutched the pen tighter.

Whatever she had to share would not cast her client in the best light.

"Apparently, some of the guests were openly discussing the case against Trey Powers. Though I can attest he was generally a fan of the limelight, he must not have cared for the speculation circulating the ballroom. My client believes that he intentionally said some harsh things to and about her in an effort to deflect the attention from himself."

"What harsh things?" Ethan asked.

"He insinuated that Mr. and Mrs. Powers were having marital issues. He also insinuated that Mrs. Powers had married his father to gain access to a society she never would have had a foothold in on her own merit. And, of course, the privilege that comes with the kind of money and connections the Powers family enjoys."

"What does your client say about these allegations?"

"My client admits that she and her husband were no longer in the honeymoon phase of their marriage, but they were still on solid ground. Both led busy lives with interests they did not share and that often separated them. They were—" she paused here, choosing the next word carefully "—evolving," she concluded.

"Fighting?"

She shook her head. "Not according to Kayla. More of a settling-in, is the way she made it sound."

He raised an eyebrow, prompting for more.

"Mrs. Powers says they didn't fight. Apparently, his marriage to Trey's mother was somewhat…volatile, so if Kayla and Tyrone disagreed on something, he tended to walk away. I get the impression communication may have been difficult between them, but I don't—" She hesitated for a moment. "Lieutenant, I've spent a lot of time around the Powers family in the past few months. I saw nothing of an aggressive nature in the dynamic between Mr. Powers and my client. Not even passively aggressive. If anything, they took particular care with each other."

He made a quick note of that assessment, then shifted gears. He'd delve deeper when he spoke to the widow herself.

"And your take on her relationship with your now former client? You said their relationship was, uh, cordial?" he asked, drawing the word out.

In this capacity, her impressions carried more weight. She was hip-deep in the Powers family drama, but most of her immersion would have come from her defense of Trey, not Kayla.

She nodded.

"But was it contentious?"

She straightened her spine. "In all the time that I was representing Tyrone Powers the third against the allegations brought against him, I never heard him disparage or denigrate Kayla Powers," she answered carefully. "I don't believe they were close, but I never witnessed or heard of anything acrimonious between them."

"Until that night," he inserted.

Ms. Fraser nodded. "Exactly. Mrs. Powers was shocked and hurt by the things my former client said the night of the gala. And according to her, her husband had no desire to play referee between his wife and his son. They discussed it on the way home from the gala, but once they reached the house, Tyrone refused to discuss it any longer."

"And you were at the gala?" he asked, shifting gears in hopes of throwing her off her game.

It didn't work. "I was for a short time. I made my appearance, spoke to some of my colleagues and a few acquaintances, but I'm not much of a party person. I left as soon as the senator departed."

"To fly back to Washington on a private plane with your boss," he said, wanting her to be well aware he had listened carefully to everything Kayla said the previous day.

"Correct. Except Harold Dennis is not technically my boss. He's the family's attorney. We both report directly to Tyrone... Reported," she corrected. "I guess everyone is assuming Harold will handle the firm now."

"I see." He made another quick note about PP&W's structure, then shifted again. "So you missed the dustup between Trey and Kayla Powers."

"I did."

"Still, a public squabble at such an important event for the family... Add that to the insinuations Trey Powers made—I have to believe your client would have been extremely upset," he stated.

Her bright blue eyes widened slightly. "I didn't think it was your job to deal in supposition, Lieutenant."

He inclined his head to acknowledge the hit but didn't let off the gas. "She wanted you to tell me this for a reason."

"Yes. She *was* upset—both by the things Trey said about her and Tyrone's refusal to defend her. I think it's reasonable for any spouse in such a position to be upset."

"Perhaps," he conceded. "Did they go to bed... angry?"

"They went to bed...agitated," she corrected. "My client was upset and she couldn't get to sleep. Once her husband was asleep, she got up and went to the kitchen for something to drink. When she awoke the next morning, Tyrone had left for an early tee time."

"So the last time your client saw her husband alive..."

"He was snoring in his bed," she stated without hesitation.

He wrote the word *snoring* on his notepad. His gut said this wasn't the only bit of information Ms. Fraser had to share. He also couldn't shake the feeling there was something she was holding back about her client's weekend activities. Placing the pen down on the pad, he looked up expectantly.

"And?"

"And what?" she asked, her brow puckering.

"Is that all you came here to tell me this morning?"

She stared back at him, one eyebrow lifting as their gazes clashed. "I gave you a significant piece of information."

The corner of his mouth twitched, but he fought the urge to smile. She was good at this game, but so was he. "You did. As I'm sure you and your client are aware, it's always good to get out in front of the gossip before we can hear it from someone else."

She inclined her head. "Things like little tiffs at public events do have a way of coming out eventually."

"They do."

Ethan watched with interest as she shifted on the hard wooden chair. He could practically see the gears meshing in her head as she decided how best to approach whatever else she had on her mind. But he was a patient man. And he had a feeling whatever it was, it would be worth the wait.

His intuition didn't lie.

"There will also be an issue with Tyrone Powers's will," she stated coolly.

He picked up his pen again, made a note of the change in subject matter, then turned his attention back to her. His heart raced with anticipation. He could only hope his expression didn't betray his heightened interest. "His will?"

She nodded. "Mrs. Powers informed me yesterday she and her husband had new wills drawn up by a firm in Little Rock." She paused as if searching her memory, but he could tell the name was on the tip of her tongue. "The Anderson law firm—Anderson & Associates— drew up the papers and witnessed their signatures."

"Anderson & Associates," he repeated as he wrote the name out. "Why not their own firm?"

He looked up as he spoke, but immediately regretted asking the question. It hurt to have a woman as challenging as Michelle Fraser look at you as if you barely met the intellectual equivalent of a piece of used chewing gum.

"Never mind. He didn't want his firm involved," he stated flatly. "I assume you're sharing this because the new will favors your client. And the fact that it was drawn up at another firm likely indicates it will meet resistance from within PP&W."

"Correct on both counts." She gave him a small smile, and Ethan couldn't help but feel slightly vindicated. "The new document kept Trey as the primary beneficiary, but changed the secondary."

"And I assume the new beneficiary is Mrs. Powers."

"It isn't unusual to make one's spouse a party to one's estate," she replied, her tone noticeably icier than it had been. "I am told the previous iteration still had

Mr. Powers's first wife, Natalie Powers, named as successor to her son."

"Do you know if Mr. Powers had a particular reason to engage another firm?"

"According to my client, Mr. Powers was not entirely comfortable working with Harold Dennis."

"The family's attorney who is not technically your boss," he murmured as he made notes.

When he looked up, he found the corners of her mouth turned up in a smile and those brilliant blue eyes glinting with repressed humor.

"Exactly."

He lowered his pen and gave her his undivided attention. Then he asked his favorite question. "Why?"

Regret twisted his gut when her smile faded and the line bisecting her eyebrows reappeared, but he squashed the sensation. He wasn't here to make this woman happy—he was here to find out who killed two members of a very prominent family. A family who had her so ensnared in their web, it was hard to tell if she was party to their plots or hapless prey.

"Why what?"

Her response jolted him. He was used to being the one who asked questions. Still, he'd been intentionally vague, and she was an attorney. Ethan shouldn't be surprised she didn't fall for his usual tactics. So he went the direct route.

"Why does your client want me to know she and her late husband had doubts about the family attorney?"

"Because she has asked me, not Harold, to represent her."

He leaned back, purposefully softening the tension between them. "What's it to me who represents her?"

She narrowed her eyes as if testing the weight of his feigned nonchalance. "Because we both know Mr. Dennis is about to descend on this scene, and I can guarantee he won't be as cooperative and forthcoming as my client and I have been." With that, she gathered the handles of her bag and rose. "You have my contact information. My client instructed me to assure you she will continue to do everything she can to aid in your investigation."

Ethan remained seated, though it went against the very strict manners his mother had drilled into him as a child. If his years as an attorney and an investigator had taught him anything, it was the value of being willing to cede the higher ground when there was no immediate advantage to holding it. Instead, he cocked his head to the side and looked up at her, prepared to launch one last arrow in an attempt to throw her off her game.

"Except she won't tell us why she really went to the lake house."

Ms. Fraser blinked, and if someone had asked him to testify under oath, he'd swear he saw a hint of her sly smile tug at the corners of her mouth. "I told you. She was feeling vulnerable and wanted some alone time."

"Was she hoping her husband would go chasing after her?" he challenged.

She shrugged. "Perhaps. I can't really say what her hopes were. I only know what she has told me."

"Do you believe her?"

"Does it matter?" she shot back.

He liked the way she handled herself so nimbly. As much as he wanted to catch her flat-footed, she managed to parry each attempt he made. A part of him wished he could go up against her in court.

"Your messages have been delivered, Ms. Fraser," he said, inclining his head with mock deference. "If your client asks how it went, tell her I gave you top marks across the board. I don't know this Harold Dennis from a hole in the wall, but I cannot imagine he'd be half as fierce as you."

She gave a little snort as she hitched her bag onto her arm. "Don't underestimate Hal Dennis, Lieutenant. Men don't end up in positions like his accidentally."

"You mean he grew up aspiring to be seated at the right hand?" he asked, but his jovial tone came across as snide, even to his own ears.

"Sometimes a strong right hand wields more power than a figurehead." She turned to leave the tiny office, her shoulders squared. "Thank you for your time."

"Thank you for your cooperation," he returned, matching her flippancy.

She glanced back. "You mean my *client*'s cooperation," she said, flashing a tight smile that didn't reach those icy eyes. "I counseled against bringing you more information. I told her to let you do your job."

"I'd expect nothing less from a good defense attorney." Pausing for a moment, he gave her an insincere smirk he'd been told was nothing less than condescending. "And I hear you're the best in town."

"Oh, isn't that nice. I'll miss Special Agent Reed. Bless her heart, she worked so hard to bring a case against Trey Powers, and now..." She heaved a sigh. "Let me know if my client can be of further assistance, Lieutenant. Happy hunting," she added, almost as an afterthought.

He sat frozen for a moment, too stunned by those last

two words to do anything but watch her wend her way through the maze of cubicles beyond his precious door.

Happy hunting.

A shiver ran up his spine and prickled his scalp. He ran his hand through his hair, trying to calm the sensation as his mind raced.

That wasn't something attorneys said to one another. The lawyers didn't come into play until after the police had done their job. She was exhorting him to do his. And not only because her client was their prime suspect.

He'd wager money Michelle Fraser had once been a hunter as well. Not for game, but for bad guys. But not only had she switched from law enforcement to the practice of law, she'd gone over to the dark side.

An occurrence even more rare than a lawyer stepping into cop shoes.

Reaching for his phone, he called Special Agent Grace Reed again. She was the one who'd planted this seed in his mind. Now, Michelle Fraser was standing between his office and the apprehension of a possible murderer. Again.

"Scott here," he said when she answered. "Listen, how deep did you dig on your background on Michelle Fraser?"

"Well, I ran a background check, of course," she began hesitantly. "Verified her credentials with the bar, studied some of her more recent cases, but I didn't go much deeper," she admitted.

He nodded his approval as she spoke. She'd done nothing more than he would have in compiling a basic dossier on counsel for the defense. "Right, why would you?" he interjected.

"Do you think I should have?"

"No, but I do think your observation about her acting more like a cop than a lawyer is spot-on. Kayla Powers has retained her to be her personal attorney."

There was a beat of silence. "She has?"

"Yes."

"Not Harold Dennis?"

"No," he confirmed.

"Interesting," Grace responded.

Ethan smiled as he heard the sound of a pen tapping travel through the line. "Isn't it?"

"Harold Dennis will not like that," she concluded, and he could almost see her turning the implications over in her mind.

"Mrs. Powers claims her husband didn't trust Mr. Dennis entirely," Ethan informed her.

Agent Reed barked a short, bitter laugh. "They did a good impression of presenting a united front whenever I saw them."

"I'd like to dig deeper on Ms. Fraser and Mr. Dennis. Do you have time to help me?"

He heard the soft intake of breath on the other end of the call and sensed that he'd caught the usually sure-footed agent off guard. Probably because he could have ordered her to help, but that wasn't Ethan's leadership style. He'd heard tales of his predecessor's bullying. But Ethan believed one got the best out of people when they operated from a position of empowerment, not fear.

"I, uh, yes," she said, quickly recovering. "Yes, Chief. I'd love to help."

"Thanks. I appreciate it. I have my hands full up here, and I know there's no one better suited to be my backup on this," he said, meaning every word.

Up until the previous day, Agent Grace Reed had

been their resident expert in all things Powers-related. He wasn't about to waste those months of work simply because his boss made a decision based on pressure and politics.

"Thank you, Agent Reed. I know the events of the past couple days must feel like a bad case of whiplash, but I promise you, I know who my best resource is on this, and I don't squander resources. Follow your nose on Fraser. Maybe she's from a family of cops? Whatever. It's early days so we don't have much to go on except gossip and our guts at this point, but I'd rather listen to intuition than a bunch of opinions from people with agendas."

"Gotcha. I'm on it," she said, and he smiled at hearing her usual brisk confidence restored.

"Thanks. I'll be in touch."

Ethan ended the call and leaned back in the chair, grasping his wrist and raising his joined hands to his forehead as he closed his eyes. He replayed the entire encounter with Michelle Fraser, trying to put his finger on exactly what it was about her that made his neurons fire. Sure, she was physically attractive. Striking in both her style and manner. But Agent Reed was right about the cop signals.

Happy hunting.

He smiled as he lowered his hands and sat up slowly, wondering if the intriguing Ms. Fraser knew those two simple words might have put her dead center in his crosshairs.

Chapter Six

The door to Powers, Powers & Walton was lettered with tasteful script. It had barely closed behind her when the firm's receptionist, Bailey, chirped, "Hold, please," into her headset and rose from her chair to catch Michelle.

"Mr. Dennis asked to see you in his office as soon as you came in," the fresh-faced young woman informed her in a grave tone.

Michelle fought the urge to smirk at the "Mr. Dennis" portion of the message. It had taken Harold Dennis weeks to break the young woman of the habit of referring to him as "Uncle Hal" to associates and clients alike. Then, she'd explain how Harold Dennis wasn't really her uncle, but that he'd known her mama and daddy, "Like forever," so he was *like* an uncle.

"Thank you, Bailey," she said as she breezed past the young woman's command console. "I'll put my things away and head up to his office now. If you'll let him know?" she called over her shoulder.

"Sure will," Bailey replied, reverting to her usual chipper disposition. As if the firm's founder and his son hadn't been discovered murdered the day before.

Michelle nodded a few hellos but didn't break stride, her eyes fixed on her office door. The more senior at-

torneys kept offices on the upper floor, so she knew
she had a little time before her presence was expected.
But she could feel the gazes of the other employees lin-
gering on her back. They couldn't know about Kayla's
decision to choose her over Harold Dennis, so she assumed they were waiting to hear if she had any insights
about the murders themselves. She almost made it to
her door before one worked up the nerve to ask directly.

"Michelle," a young man called out to her in a voice
so raspy it broke.

She fought the urge to cringe. Chet Barrow was
as obnoxious and entitled as his friend Trey had been
but lacked a filter and self-awareness. Something that
worked against him, both at work and as Trey's ally.
Still, he was a bright attorney when he applied himself, and the guy did sound truly upset over the loss
of his friend.

Her hand gripping the door handle, she turned to find
the ambitious young attorney standing beside her, un-
characteristically disheveled, all traces of feigned cool
stripped away. She couldn't help softening toward him.

Chet had followed Trey around like a puppy. Em-
ulated almost everything Trey was or did, from his
haircut to his choices in shoes and neckties. The only
difference was that while Chet came from a family with
some money, he didn't have the seemingly unlimited
funding the Powerses did. Which meant he didn't have
exactly the same expensive wristwatch and cuff links
the police believed would help prove Trey Powers had
killed Mallory Murray.

"Hey, Chet," she said by way of greeting. "How are
you holding up?"

He shook his head, and his perfectly coiffed hair

flopped over his wrinkled brow. "I just can't... I can't wrap my head around it."

"I know," she replied with genuine sympathy. Opening the door to her office, she strode to her desk, knowing Chet would follow her in.

"It's just so unreal."

Michelle didn't bother telling him she'd been at the crime scene with Kayla Powers and it was all very real. Everyone would know that by now. She placed the tote that contained her laptop in the bottom drawer of her desk, then opened the center drawer and withdrew a key she palmed under a container of breath mints.

"I know. I have to head upstairs to meet with Hal right now," she explained, pulling a face to convey the dread she truly felt. She popped a mint into her mouth, tossed the container back into the drawer, then locked the desk down as if she did so every time she stepped away from her office. "Can I catch up with you later?"

"Oh. Yeah. Sure," he said, backing out of the office as she moved toward the door.

She slipped the key into the pocket of her jacket, then offered a wan smile. "Thanks. I hate to give you the rush, but I'm sure Bailey has already informed Uncle Hal that I'm on the premises, so..."

The use of the nickname the associates had adopted the first time it slipped from Bailey's lips made the corners of Chet's mouth twitch. "Right. Better get up there," he said, stepping aside as she pulled her office door closed behind them.

She didn't bother locking it. The notes she'd been accumulating about the firm and the defense of both Trey and Kayla Powers were in the bag she took everywhere and secured in the locked desk. "I'll check in with you later," she said, but she didn't mean it.

Michelle had every intention of avoiding interaction with as many people as possible. She'd spoken to her intermediary with the Bureau the night before and they agreed time was of the essence. The Powers family tragedy would play out as it needed to with or without her. She'd get what she needed from the firm's database and get the heck out of there as soon as possible.

Heads swiveled away, and people tried to pretend they weren't trying to catch any snippet of conversation they could. Michelle lifted a hand in farewell, then headed for the open-riser staircase that led to the second floor of the building. The entire interior of the PP&W offices had been renovated many times since it was first established, but the firm held onto the essence of the sleek mid-century modern design of the building. The staircase was a testament to that aesthetic. The soles of her pumps clicked on the mica-flecked faux marble installed sometime during the Kennedy administration. Now, sleek cables provided support for the staircase, but from old photographs she knew that once upon a time the spindles had mimicked the curved rails used around the reception area.

The second floor was comprised of four large corner offices, each with a seating area for an assistant, and comfortable couches for clients to relax on while they waited.

She turned left and walked toward the office on the southeast corner of the building. Its view was the least desirable of the four, but it still beat the street level parking lot view most of the lower floor's offices provided.

Harold's longtime assistant, Nancy, was seated at her

post. When Michelle approached, the older woman nodded and said, "Go on in. He's expecting you."

"Thank you," Michelle said, flashing a quick smile.

She wrapped two knuckles against the door and turned the handle. "You wanted to see me?" she asked as she poked her head through the opening.

Harold Dennis stood from his chair, motioning her forward with one hand while he clutched the receiver of his desk phone in the other. She entered the office and closed the door quietly behind her, staying near the opposite side of the room until he finished his phone call.

"Sorry about that," he said, placing the phone back on the cradle.

"No problem." Michelle started forward.

Harold came out from behind the desk, extending both hands as if to embrace her. Her steps faltered. While they had a cordial working relationship, they certainly weren't on hugging terms. Then again, two of the firm's own had never been murdered before.

Thankfully, Harold stopped short of a full-on hug, instead gripping only her upper arms and giving them a gentle squeeze. "This is just horrible," he said, shaking his head.

"Yes," Michelle agreed. She looked up and noticed that his salt-and-pepper hair had been freshly barbered. Searching her memory, she tried to recall if he looked this perfectly groomed at the gala just a few days before.

"I keep trying to think of something more to say about it, but for the first time in my life, I'm at a complete loss for words," he admitted. He gestured her toward one of the leather upholstered chairs situated in front of his massive desk, and Michelle wordlessly accepted the invitation to sit. To her surprise, Hal dropped down into the other chair rather than resuming his spot behind the desk.

"I can't imagine how it must have been for you and Kayla," he said, his voice dripping with concerned sympathy.

"I won't lie, it was pretty shocking," she confessed. "You know I've seen a lot of things, crime scene photos, that sort of thing." She shuddered. "I've even been on a few scenes, but never one so…" The word *fresh* sprang to mind, but she didn't care to use it. It implied a shorter timeline than would behoove her client. "Active," she said at last.

"No doubt," he said, nodding along. "I can't believe it."

Michelle couldn't help noticing he didn't seem to have even a hint of a suntan. No time, maybe? Had he gotten off the plane, gone directly to accommodations only to hole up with his laptop on what was supposed to be a vacation? He would have had at least a full day to enjoy the beach and all the splashy sunshine of Barbados. Even if he were an ardent sunscreen user, surely he would have picked up some color. A slightly sunburned nose, a pink line along the part in his meticulously styled hair?

"And of course, I saw Kayla this morning," Hal stated, interrupting her line of thought.

"Did you?" She shouldn't have been surprised that he would go directly to Mrs. Powers upon his return, but Michelle couldn't recall telling him where her client had been staying.

"Kayla called me and told me that she would feel more comfortable with you representing her in this matter." His tone was matter-of-fact, but Michelle heard a slight edge in his statement.

"I hope you don't mind. I'm certainly happy to step back if you have an objection, but I think in this case she feels more comfortable talking to a woman." It was a nonsensical argument given the situation, but one that Michelle often found effective when dealing with men. Particularly men of the previous generation. Once she played the woman-to-woman card, they generally backed off pretty quickly.

"Yes." He blinked twice, then nodded. "And it would be very difficult for me, given how close Tyrone and I were."

Michelle did nothing to give away her doubts on that particular topic. "Yes, she mentioned that to me. She doesn't want to put you in a difficult position."

"Well, I know that with you she has the most brilliant counsel PP&W has to offer," he said with an ingratiating smile. "Otherwise, we wouldn't have entrusted you with young Trey's defense."

He closed his eyes and let out a heavy sigh. "It's impossible to believe he's gone as well."

Michelle kept any snarky commentary about Trey Powers's escape from justice to herself. She, more than anyone, was supposed to presume the young man had been innocent until proven guilty.

Then, like magic, Harold sat up straight, his expression clearing of all hints of sadness and becoming all business. "Kayla tells me you've met with the gentleman from the Criminal Investigation Division." It wasn't a question but a statement of fact.

"Yes. His name is Ethan Scott. Lieutenant. Apparently, he's Grace Reed's direct supervisor."

Dennis, having been involved in all the pre-arrest interviews between Special Agent Reed and Trey Powers, was well acquainted with the other agent's name. "Ah, I see."

"As such, I think it's safe to assume he has access to all of the information the CID gathered in the investigation of Trey in the Murray case. I am also of the opinion they'll be looking at the family dynamic with a somewhat jaundiced eye."

Hal inclined his head. "I agree. Go on."

"Against my counsel, Kayla Powers submitted to voluntary testing for gunshot residue, fingerprinting, clothing analysis and has made it clear that she intends to cooperate with the state police investigation in any way she can."

"Going over the top to prove her innocence," Hal commented dryly.

"I believe she *is* innocent. I think she's submitting whatever evidence she can provide to clear her name in hopes that the police will move past the obvious spouse as suspect and move on in their investigation into who may have done this to Tyrone and Trey."

"Yes, time is of the essence," Hal agreed, though his expression remained stony. "Not only do we need to see the killer brought to justice, but we also want to mitigate any blowback this may have against the firm."

Michelle's surprise must have shown on her face before she could mask it.

"Ms. Fraser, Michelle, you know that I'm good friends...was good friends..." He drew a deep breath, then plowed on. "I am good friends," he asserted at last, "with both William and Tyrone Powers. And as their friend I owe it to both of them to be sure that the family firm and the legacy it was intended to be for both Tyrone's and William's sons continues untarnished."

"Of course."

"I don't mean to sound unfeeling, you understand, but I do also have a responsibility to look to the future and to guard our presence."

"Yes. I understand."

"You'll keep me apprised of any further contact between Mrs. Powers and Lieutenant Scott? Or any other member of law enforcement, for that matter?"

Michelle heard the note of finality in the question and placed her hands on the chair arms to rise. "Yes, sir."

"Thank you for taking this on," Hal said as he rose as well. "I know that your expertise will be a great comfort to Kayla in the days to come."

Michelle nodded. "I'll be in touch with the coroner's office about when they might be able to release the bodies so that arrangements can be made."

"Thank you again."

Anxious to escape, Michelle skirted the chair and headed directly for the door. But before she could turn the handle, he called after her. "Of course, in this case we may have to start the process of distributing Ty's responsibilities and assets. I know we have a copy of his will on file. We'll have to make arrangements for a smooth transference of management."

Michelle froze for a moment, then turned back to him, ready to test the waters. "I assume you'll be acting as managing partner in the interim?"

"Me?" He chuckled and shook his head. "Oh, no, that will fall on young Del's shoulders, I'm afraid. But

I will be here to provide advice and counsel as needed," he added with a reassuring smile.

"Oh, yes, Del."

She wasn't surprised to hear that William's son would be considered next in line to manage the firm, but she thought Hal Dennis might possibly use this opportunity to make a power move. She'd been wrong. Doing her best to keep her expression neutral, she nodded and twisted the door handle. "Yes, I'll make certain he knows that I'm here to help in any way."

"Thank you, Michelle."

With that, she made her escape. Her pumps clattered on the marble steps as she hurried back to her office, but she didn't bother shifting her weight to her toes to muffle the noise. She had a lot of work to do and not very much time to accomplish it all. This moment of transition could prove to be critical in both of her cases. She needed to act now, while the firm operated in a vacuum of grief and uncertainty. This would be her best chance to catch them in the act.

Back in her office, she unlocked her desk, opened the drawer and extracted her laptop. She logged in, but rather than opening one of the many legal documents that populated the screen as the system awoke, she typed in a command that allowed her to access the network's operating system.

Working in incognito mode so her digital footprints would be covered, she logged into the financial database where the firm's financial transactions were stored. The pattern she'd been following for the past nine months appeared to be uninterrupted. She exhaled in relief. She was able to retrieve the same information using a remote access key, but doing so off-site left a digital footprint larger than a yeti.

While she was here in the office, she was just another attorney logged into the network. The next few days would be crucial. If the pattern didn't change in the wake of Tyrone Powers's death, it could signal that he—and for that matter, his son—were not involved in the fiscal malfeasance she'd uncovered. After all, dead men could do no bad deeds. That would narrow her list of suspects precipitously. And, if Kayla's assertion that Hal Dennis was more William's man on the inside checked out, it might give her the firepower she needed to prove her case.

Logging out of the operating system, she slid back into defense attorney mode. Opening the file she'd begun on Kayla's behalf, she started typing up notes about her meeting with Lieutenant Scott earlier that morning while they were still fresh in her mind.

Fifteen minutes passed before she was interrupted.

"Knock knock," a male voice called from the open doorway.

Michelle looked up to find Delray Powers standing on her threshold. On instinct, she lowered the laptop screen as she rose from her chair. "Oh, come in, Del," she said to cover her shock at seeing him there. Only then did it occur to her that she should have thought to visit him following her meeting with Harold Dennis. Then again, she and Del had never had very much interaction other than some mildly friendly chit-chat. Still, condolences were in order, and she'd blown right past them.

"I'm so sorry," she said sincerely. "I should have come to see you—"

"No worries," he assured her, his voice creaking a lit-tle bit. "I just got here myself. Uncle Hal suggested that I come down here and…" he trailed off with a shrug. "I guess reassure people?"

Michelle's heart went out to the young man. He wasn't even thirty by her best guess, but now the weight of this firm would rest squarely on his shoulders. At least for a few days. A part of her couldn't help wondering how he'd react when Tyrone's new will was revealed.

"Of course." She crossed the room and extended her hand. When he took it, she enclosed his with her other hand. This was about as touchy-feely as she was will-ing to get with a colleague she barely knew. "I am so sorry about your uncle. And Trey, of course. I know you two were close."

A lie. Trey had been nothing but disdainful toward his cousin, but now was not the time to poke at old wounds.

"Thank you."

The bewildered expression on the young man's face told her the response was prompted by ingrained man-ners more than genuine gratitude for her condolences. He clearly had no idea what to say beyond those two words, and she had nothing more to offer than the usual platitudes.

"I know you're probably feeling overwhelmed," she said, taking a step toward the door. When he backed up, she fought the urge to smile. He wanted out of this conversation as much as she did. "If there's anything I can do to help…"

"Uncle Hal says you're representing Kayla," he stated flatly.

"He called me the minute he got off the phone with

Kayla and asked me to step in and help...handle things. I assured him—and now you as well—that I will do my best to keep the firm's name separate from the family's personal tragedy as much as I possibly can."

"Thank you," he said again.

Michelle saw no reason to draw things out. "I know you must have so much to do. Thank you for coming in. Your presence will be a comfort to the associates."

As if awoken from a daze, he nodded eagerly. "Yes, I, uh, I was going to go on and, um, make the rounds."

She inclined her head. "Of course. Please let me know if there's anything more I can do to help."

With another somber nod, Del backed away, lifting his hand in an awkward half wave. She counted to ten before walking to the door to be certain he'd moved on. When she spotted a cluster of Trey Powers's sycophants gathered around the cousin her late client had openly mocked, she closed her office door without a qualm.

Then she locked it.

There was work to do and a power struggle on the horizon. Her days at PP&W would be numbered regardless of who was in charge, and she refused to leave without getting what she came for.

Reaching into the depths of her tote bag, she pulled out the burner phone she picked up at the local superstore on her way home from getting Kayla Powers settled at her hotel. The clock was ticking on this investigation, and she needed to update her contact at the Bureau.

Chapter Seven

Ethan dawdled as he and Sheriff Stenton followed Harold Dennis's assistant to the staircase. The first floor of Powers, Powers & Walton was abuzz with purpose. The hubbub was a marked difference from the hushed silence of the executive level where he'd met with Tyrone Powers's family attorney. He scanned the warren of desks in the open-floor-plan office, but his gaze didn't linger on the bullpen for too long. Michelle Fraser was not a cubicle dweller. She had to be behind one of the many closed doors encircling the open office space. As if he conjured her, one of those doors opened and she stepped into the corridor. His steps slowed as she turned in his direction.

Had someone told her he was on-site, or was this mere coincidence?

"Excuse me for one moment, please," he said to the woman leading them down the last of the steps. "I'd like to have a word with Ms. Fraser, if I may."

The sheriff glanced back up the staircase, then at Harold Dennis's assistant, his expression wary and his posture uneasy. "Do you need me to come along?"

Ethan shook his head. "No, thank you. I know you have a lot to do. Don't let me keep you." He offered the older woman an ingratiating smile. "I can see myself out from here. Thank you again for your time and your assistance, Mrs. Ayers."

He and Sheriff Stenton had questioned her along with her boss. Dennis was the only one of the firm's senior lawyers in the office. According to Mr. Dennis, William Powers would be arriving in town later in the afternoon.

"Oh, it's just Nancy," she said, giving his arm an absentminded pat. "And please let me know if I can be of any further help," she assured him. "It's so hard to believe," she repeated for what had to be the tenth time. She pressed the crumpled tissue she balled in her fist to her nose and glanced away.

Ethan tipped his head down to acknowledge her pain. "I know, and we are so sorry to have to impose on you at such a time. I'm sure you understand. Every minute is a precious commodity in a case such as this."

"Absolutely," she said in her soft drawl. She gestured toward Ms. Fraser, then turned her attention to the sheriff. "I'll see you out, Bud, uh, I mean, Sheriff."

"Much obliged," the older man replied without missing a beat.

Ethan and Stenton exchanged nods and farewell, both knowing they'd be meeting again sooner rather than later. When he started for Michelle Fraser's door, she began walking in his direction, meeting him halfway. For a moment he wondered if there might be a reason she didn't want him to come to her private office. Surely, she knew it would be better if the two of them were to speak in private.

No sooner had the thought formed, she swept an arm to her right in a gesture of invitation. "Lieutenant Scott," she said by way of greeting. "Please come inside."

Ethan turned and saw she was inviting him into a small conference room. A glass wall exposed a table large enough to seat six people comfortably, eight in a crunch. There was a small bar at the room with a built-in mini fridge and a single-serving coffee maker.

He followed her into the room.

"Can I offer you a cup of coffee? Some water?" she asked as if he were a client coming in for a consultation.

"No, thank you. I had a cup upstairs as I was meeting with Mr. Dennis."

She nodded and pulled out a chair and gestured for him to do the same. "I thought perhaps you might come in to see him this morning," she said in a neutral tone. "Things have been fairly strained around here today, as you can imagine."

"I would expect them to be," he said evenly. "Have you spoken to your client again since this morning?"

She gave her head a brief shake and stopped as if uncertain she was giving the correct answer. "Not since I've spoken to you," she confirmed, holding his gaze steady. "Why? Is there something I need to discuss with her?"

"No, not necessarily." Ethan took in the view of the Benton County courthouse afforded by the narrow floor-to-ceiling windows. "The state crime lab sent back a report on the gunpowder residue and clothing. It's preliminary, of course, but there were no surprises."

"By no surprises you mean—" she left the sentence hanging.

He lifted a shoulder in a shrug. "We both know gunshot residue testing is highly inaccurate in most cases. The only thing it proves conclusively is the person submitting to the testing had been in the vicinity of a gun-powder discharge."

"And my client has not been in the vicinity of a gun-powder discharge," she asserted.

"The tests confirmed as much."

"And the bloodstains on her clothing? The testing confirmed the blood was smeared onto her clothes, but not fresh, am I correct?"

It was his turn to nod. "Correct."

"And since we've stipulated the presence of my client's fingerprints in the room where the victims were discovered, it's difficult to prove she had anything to do with their deaths. In the absence of a weapon, that is," she amended, lifting a single eyebrow as if challenging him to produce a weapon.

A part of Ethan wished he could, if only to wipe her smile off her face. But unfortunately, not one shred of the evidence they'd collected thus far pointed to Kayla Powers as the murderer.

"I assume you've asked your client to compile a list of people who may hold grudges against either her late husband or Trey Powers."

"I have." She folded her hands on the table in front of her. "I have to imagine we have a number of the same names on our list. Perhaps we should collaborate, Lieu-tenant, rather than work around or against each other."

Ethan eyed her cautiously. This wasn't the first time a defense attorney had tried to go with the useful and cooperative ploy to mask their client's sins. But both he and the sheriff agreed they did not believe the widow had anything to do with these grisly deaths. Of course, their personal opinions didn't mean they weren't going to continue to look at her long and hard.

"We would appreciate any and all cooperation you can give," he said neutrally.

"I think you'll find we've been more cooperative than most people in my client's position would have been."

"Most people don't have the privilege of having an attorney on-site almost immediately upon the discovery of a crime," he shot back.

"Ah, but I was only called in to offer emotional support. You forget, my client is an attorney herself."

"Isn't there some saying about the attorney who represents themselves having a fool for a client?" he asked, certain the jab would hit home with her.

"There absolutely is. But my client didn't retain herself as an attorney, she retained me. But I can assure you even in those harrowing moments before I was able to get to the scene—well, Mrs. Powers is a bright woman who knows how to handle herself."

"So, you'll share your list with me?" he asked, hoping the change in tactic would throw her off-balance enough to catch her off guard.

No such luck.

"I already said we would, Lieutenant,"

"If we're working in a spirit of cooperation, can we drop the formalities? I'm Ethan." He leaned in, locking gazes with her. "May I call you Michelle?"

"Absolutely," she said easily.

He sat there, momentarily transfixed by her piercing blue eyes.

"My client has nothing to hide," she stated boldly.

"I don't believe your client is guilty of these murders. But I do believe she's hiding something. I believe you may be as well." He leaned back as he waited for her to digest both simple statements. He could almost see the cogs turning in her mind. "What is your client not saying?"

"I cannot tell you without her permission, but I can assure you it has nothing to do with the commission of this crime."

Instinct told him she was being truthful, but all assurance aside, they both knew the lack of a better suspect left Kayla Powers at the top of his list.

"Okay, so I'm listening. Tell me—who do you think might possibly have a motive to do this?" he challenged.

She leaned back in her chair and drew a deep breath, letting it go slowly and deliberately. "Honestly? If he weren't one of the victims, I would have said Trey Powers," she confessed in a low tone.

"He was your client," he challenged.

"Yes. In a different case. And I think we both know Agent Reed did an excellent job of piling up enough circumstantial evidence to bring him to court, but I doubt whether the government could have proven their case beyond a reasonable doubt."

"And now we'll never know," he said grimly.

"Correct. We will never know."

"Off the record, and for what it's worth—there is no record anymore since the prime suspect is now deceased— do you think he did it?"

"Killed Mallory Murray?" she asked.

It was a stalling tactic and they both knew it, so he waited her out.

"I believe Ms. Murray met an untimely death on Table Rock Lake while boating with Trey Powers," she said, choosing each word with exacting care. "I believe she was knocked off the boat by a blow to the head.

And I believe no attempt to rescue her from the lake was made."

"So you would go with negligent homicide," he said in summation. "Do you think she fell off or was knocked off?"

"I have no idea." She gave her head a slow shake. "Of course I have seen the reports from the crime lab, the coroner and the reconstruction by experts, but I still can't say for certain. I don't think any jury would have been able to convict him of more than negligence."

"Though he purposely drove the boat back to the family slip, swore his coworkers to secrecy and claimed not to have seen the victim the night she disappeared?" he pressed.

"All moot points. He'll never be tried for this case now. And likely, Mallory Murray's brother will never find any satisfaction within the judicial system." She tucked her chin to her chest, then shook her head. "It doesn't make me happy. I've met Matthew Murray. He's a nice man and a good prosecutor. I know he and his sister were not close, but no one deserves to lose a family member under such circumstances."

Ethan placed his hands together and leaned in. "So, we can't point the finger at Trey, and Mrs. Powers is presumably exonerated, at the moment." He added the last with a direct stare. "Who's next on the list?"

He watched as Michelle Fraser chewed the inside of her cheek. It was actually the first time he'd seen her look nervous about anything, and it intrigued him.

At last, she cast a pointed look at the ceiling. Ethan did his best to keep a straight face. "Somebody here at the firm?" he asked cautiously.

"It's possible. I told you the deceased and my client

had drawn up revised wills. My client believes some of the members of senior management would not be pleased by his directives."

"And by not pleased, you mean royally ticked off." Ethan rocked back on the chair, hooking his arm over the edge of the seat back. Was she accusing one of two men with seemingly airtight alibis of double homicide? "But how? Mr. Dennis was in Barbados, and Senator Powers on the other side of the world."

"Has anyone checked the flight plans?" she asked. "Do we know for certain Harold Dennis ever landed in Barbados?" Folding her arms in front of her she gripped her elbows as she leaned closer to the table. "I'm told the corporate jet they borrowed had already returned to Arkansas. He claims he flew commercial home, which is why it took him so long to get back. If the jet had waited there, he could have been back within hours of Kayla Powers discovering the bodies. Instead, he had to wait for a flight."

She said the last part with enough derision to make his ears prick out. Michelle Fraser didn't like Harold Dennis. Oh, it was nothing overt, but something in the way she spoke of him made her irritation more apparent than she would probably like.

"I will make a note to follow up with the client who loaned the senator and Mr. Dennis the jet for the trip," he assured her as he pulled his phone from his pocket and quickly typed a reminder to do so.

"Anyone—"

A rising crescendo of voices bounced off the glass. He and Michelle turned in unison toward the front of the office in time to see an immaculately dressed woman clad all in black enveloped in a stout hug by Nancy

Ayers. Even though the woman was locked in Nancy's embrace, Ethan got a decent look at her. Tasteful but expensive jewelry, a rock the size of hail on her hand and artfully streaked hair twisted into an elaborate yet sedate style. The associates hung back, but some of the older members of the PP&W staff pressed forward.

"Oh, here we go," Michelle said under her breath. "Here's one for your list," she said, turning her attention back to him.

"Who is she?"

"Lieutenant, you're about to meet Natalie Powers Cantrell, Tyrone's ex-wife and Trey's mother."

Ethan rose, pivoting to get a better look at the woman surrounded by the staff of the firm. He couldn't help wondering if Kayla Powers would receive the same warm condolences.

As if reading his mind, Michelle gave a soft grunt of displeasure. "All hail the returning almost widow."

His head swiveled away from the crowd to the petite woman now standing beside him. "You don't like her."

"Let's say Trey didn't come by his sense of entitlement all on his own." She gave a wan smile. "Mrs. Cantrell insisted on joining a few of my meetings with Trey as we prepared his defense."

"I hear she got quite a settlement in the divorce," he said, nodding as he recalled all of the information he had on Tyrone's first wife. "And remarried, I assume?"

"Remarried well," Michelle provided. "The Cantrell family is one of Little Rock's oldest and most revered—as I am sure she'll let you know within the first five minutes of conversation," she added.

"Ah. So she took Tyrone's money then married more money."

"Money does tend to attract money. Of course, the Cantrells swim in a much larger society pond. Up here, the Powers family was at the top of the heap. I'm told in Little Rock, there's more jostling for position."

"I can imagine."

"Come, I'll introduce you," she offered, waving a hand at the glass door.

As they approached the diminishing knot of people, she leaned in and spoke softly, "I'm not exactly sure how this will go…"

Before he could respond, two of the associates jumped back as if they might be radioactive, but Nancy took a step closer to the impeccably coiffed woman. Natalie Powers Cantrell was a beautiful woman. She wore the glow of a woman decades younger, likely due in equal parts to wealth and good health. But her countenance was cool and closed off. Despite receiving so many heartfelt embraces, she carried an air of the untouchable. Perhaps it was a defense mechanism, he allowed. After all, the woman was suffering through not one, but two losses. But there was a stillness in the way she held herself that seemed off to Ethan, though he couldn't put a finger on exactly why.

"Mrs. Cantrell," Michelle said as she approached, interrupting his observations. "I am so sorry for your loss. Losses," she said, quickly correcting herself.

Ethan wondered if the slip had been a calculated one on the sharp-eyed attorney's part, but he didn't dare look away from Natalie Powers Cantrell. Something told him he needed to watch this woman closely if he wanted to catch any flicker of emotion.

"Mrs. Cantrell," he said, offering her his hand. "I am Lieutenant Ethan Scott of the Arkansas State Police Criminal Investigation Division. You have my condolences."

"Thank you." The older woman lifted her chin and looked him straight in the eye. Without looking at Michelle, she spoke in a low voice vibrating with anger. "You have some nerve, switching from defending my son to the woman who murdered him."

"Mrs. Cantrell—" Ethan began, but Michelle cut him off.

"I took the cases assigned to me by Harold Dennis," she interjected, her tone calm and soothing. As if this wasn't the first time she'd had to convey this message to the other woman. "If either Trey or Mrs. Powers felt the representation I provided was not adequate, they were free to fire me and choose another attorney."

"*Mrs.* Powers," Natalie Cantrell said, practically spitting the name from her mouth. She flashed a furious look at Michelle, then refocused her attention on him.

Ethan fought the urge to shift his weight as she gave him a once-over likely meant to make him feel like he'd been dressed down. But he stood his ground. "Mrs. Cantrell, I assure you, with the help of the local authorities, we are giving this case our full attention."

"Can you understand why one might wonder why you're here fraternizing with her—" she paused to cast Michelle a withering glare "—attorney. Such as she is."

To her credit, Michelle Fraser didn't flinch. Nor did she take the bait. Instead, she turned to him with a pleasant smile and said, "Thank you for keeping me up to date, Lieutenant. Please let me know if my client or I can further aid the investigation."

She pivoted on her heel and walked back to her office, unperturbed by the stares following her.

The woman beside him cleared her throat indelicately. When he turned back to Natalie Cantrell, he found her watching him with narrowed eyes and snapped back into business mode.

"Our investigation is ongoing," he said stiffly. "As I am sure you are aware, time is of the essence. If you wouldn't mind answering a few questions?" He glanced over at Harold Dennis's assistant, and gave her an appropriately somber nod. "We can all go back up to Mr. Dennis's office, if you would be more comfortable."

Without a response, Natalie Cantrell turned and strode toward the staircase he'd descended, leaving Ethan and Nancy to follow in her wake.

Chapter Eight

"I can't say I'm surprised," Kayla said dryly. "After all, Trey was her pride and joy."

They were seated opposite each other in the hotel suite once again, but this time, the room seemed to be strewn with Kayla Powers's possessions. If she didn't know the police still had the house cordoned off, Michelle might have wondered if she'd gone home to pack more than the overnight bag she'd left with. But then she noticed the price tag attached to the thick cashmere throw draped over the arm of the sofa.

Her client had gone out to shop, and the realization struck Michelle with a bolt of panic. She couldn't blame the woman for indulging in a little retail therapy, but the optics of a new widow out buying up creature comforts would not play well.

"Kayla, have you been shopping?" She added what she hoped came across as a playful little grimace to the end of the question to soften the judgment in her tone.

"I needed to pick up a few things. I didn't pack much and…" She trailed off as they both surveyed the room. "This place is so beige."

The impulse to scoff at such a comment coming from a woman who decorated a room in fifty shades of white was strong, but Michelle refrained. Instead, she nodded understandingly. "I get you. But maybe you should make a list of things you need and I can bring them to you?" Michelle hated the hesitancy she heard in her suggestion and pushed through it to a place of certainty. "Anything at all. I can bring it to you."

"If I'm going to be held prisoner in this room, I may as well call Lieutenant Scott and ask if they have an open cell for me," Kayla said coolly.

Michelle pulled off the kid gloves she'd been using with her client. "That's where you'll end up if people see you out shopping for anything other than a black dress."

"You said Lieutenant Scott confirmed they had no hard evidence."

"And you know as well as I do how quickly the circumstantial can pile up. You know we have to manage the narrative in order to do so."

"It's cold in here and I can't get the temperature to come up," she complained, her voice edging into whine country.

Eager to head her off, Michelle held up a hand. "I totally get it. I run a heater under my desk in the summer because they freeze me out with the A/C in the office, but it's better if you limit how much you're out in public. At least for a short time."

"One of the deputies took me to the house to collect clothes for Ty," she said quietly.

"But, the coroner—" Michelle began.

"I know, but I had to do *something*," Kayla insisted. "Anyhow, I looked in my closet and realized I have black cocktail dresses, but nothing appropriate for funeral services."

"I see." Michelle softened her tone. "So, you went

shopping for a dress and figured you'd pick up some other things while you were out. Makes sense."

Kayla bit her lip and looked away. "I don't know if I can go back there again. The house," she clarified in a whisper.

"Understandable."

"And I know this place is temporary, but I needed something to make it feel less…" She ran her hand over the plush throw, tears welling in her eyes. "I know I shouldn't be out shopping. I know better."

Michelle softened. "I get it. You wanted something to feel normal. Comfortable."

"Nothing will ever be normal again," Kayla said flatly.

"A new normal," Michelle suggested.

"I hate that saying," Kayla snapped.

Done coddling her client for the day, Michelle pressed her hands to her knees and rose. "Okay, fine. Well, you do know better. If there's anything you need, text me a list."

Agitated, Kayla twisted the glittering ring Tyrone Powers had placed on her finger. "I'm trapped here."

"No, you are free to come and go as you please. But keeping a low profile is a better strategy for keeping those freedoms in place." She picked up her bag, and hoisted it onto her shoulder. "Harold Dennis said something about needing to read the will sooner rather than later in order to ensure a smooth transition for the firm. I don't think he has any idea about the revisions made."

"If Natalie is here, and William arriving today, they will likely move on to probate the will before the bodies are even released. Ghouls," she added, reaching for the bottle of water she'd placed on the side table.

Michelle sank back down into the chair. "Do you have access to a copy of the new will?"

"I asked the firm we used in Little Rock to send a copy via courier."

"Excellent."

"They'll challenge its validity," she said grimly. "They'll say I drew it up and forged Ty's signature without his knowledge."

"Most likely, but you said there was also a copy in Tyrone's office safe. If they try to reject the document, we can always go to Tyrone's safe. You haven't been in there recently, have you?"

She shook her head. "No. Truthfully, I avoided going to PP&W after Ty and I married. It was too uncomfortable. For everyone," she added.

"Because you went from colleague to the boss's wife."

"Not many people knew about my relationship with Ty before we got married."

"And you didn't have a big wedding?"

She shook her head. "No. Our families. Plus Harold, of course."

"Of course."

"Judge Walton performed the ceremony."

"And it took place at…"

"The lake house." She gave a rueful smile. "Until Trey got into trouble, I thought of it as a place where happy things happened." She glanced down at her ring, then back up again. "I had my first real conversation with Ty there." Her bottom lip quivered, but she held it together. "He had a cookout and I'd won a case for a friend of his, so he invited me. I don't think he believed I'd actually show up, but…"

"You did."

"I did."

"And the rest was history," Michelle concluded.

"People don't believe it, but the rest was a love story." She paused as if considering her point. "Except those are supposed to have a happy ending, aren't they?"

Exhaling loudly, Michelle looked her client straight in the eye. "I believe you, and I promise I'm doing my best to get you the happiest possible outcome under the circumstances."

Kayla slumped in capitulation. "I know you are. I'll stay put unless I clear it with you first."

Michelle stood again, her tote still clutched to her side. "I'm not your mother or your keeper. I'm your attorney, and as such I advise you to focus on making arrangements for your husband. You can figure out what comes next in terms of where you'll live and what you'll do later. Let's focus on getting through this week. Okay?"

Kayla nodded. "Yes. Okay. Good plan."

Feeling far more reassured than she thought she'd be, Michelle started for the door. "I'll check in with Lieutenant Scott in the morning, if I don't hear from him sooner."

"Okay," came the dull, but compliant, response from behind her.

"And, Kayla," Michelle said, pausing with her hand on the door handle and looking back. "Watch the wine. I have a feeling we're both going to need all our wits to run this gauntlet. We need to make sure everyone is looking for the real killer." She waited until her client turned to meet her gaze. "You can fall apart later, if you need to."

"Oh, I'll need to," Kayla said with a short, harsh laugh. "But I'll wait."

Their gazes met and held. Michelle saw the sharp, savvy attorney who'd captured Tyrone Powers's heart. "I have a feeling you're stronger than you give yourself credit for being," she announced as she opened the hotel room door. "I'll call you later."

She pulled her phone from her bag as she hurried down the corridor to the elevator. She was composing a text to her paralegal at PP&W when she stepped off at the lobby two minutes later.

"Ms. Fraser! Michelle!" someone shouted the second her heel hit the tile floor.

"There she is," another voice called.

The sound of hurried footsteps pulled her attention from the phone's small screen. But as she watched the small knot of reporters approach, phones and recorders in hand, she quickly looked down again.

"Is it true you're representing Kayla Powers?" one called out as she tried to speed walk past them.

"Isn't that a conflict of interest since you were counsel for one of the victims?"

"What does Senator Powers think about your defending Mrs. Powers?"

She kept walking, only peeking out from under her brows to be sure she was on course for the most direct route to the front door.

"Senator Powers arrived this afternoon, but there's been no indication he's paid Mrs. Powers a visit," a persistent young man said, pressing in close as he jostled alongside her, his phone thrust directly under her chin. When she stumbled over one of his feet, she had to grab onto the reporter on the opposite side to keep from going down. Drawing to an abrupt halt, she took advantage of their surprise to straighten her shoulders and collect herself. She waited there on the all-weather mat inside the hotel until she was sure she had the undivided attention of the reporter who'd tripped her and all his colleagues before speaking.

Looking down at the recording devices thrust into her personal space, she waited until a full five seconds had ticked by before opening her mouth.

"There is an active and ongoing investigation of a tragic double homicide taking place. I have no comment beyond that," she said succinctly.

Then, she pushed through their outstretched arms and strode out the door, practically daring members of the media assembled in the nondescript lobby to try to read something into her simple statement.

She got into her car and locked the doors. Thankfully, none of the reporters had followed her out. They knew who their quarry was. They wanted a shot at the widow, not the lawyer.

She started the car, adjusted the air vents to blow on her heated face, then exhaled long and loud. Taking a moment, she shot a quick text to Kayla warning her about the media camped out in the lobby. Then, sliding low in the driver's seat, she rummaged in her bag until her fingers closed around her second mobile phone. She placed a call to her contact, but when someone knocked on her window, she jabbed so hard at the button to end the call that the phone squirted from her grasp and tumbled to the floorboard.

Looking up, she found Ethan Scott staring down at her, his brow furrowed with concern. Michelle glanced nervously back at the hotel entrance, then lowered her window a crack. Gesturing to the passenger seat of her car, she said, "Quick, get in."

Those thick brows shot straight for his hairline. "Get in?"

"There are reporters in there," she explained in a rush. "Get in and we can talk without someone seeing us."

He complied without argument. While he circled the car, she grabbed her bag from the seat she'd offered to him and shoved it to the floor between her legs. She'd have to find the burner phone later. And pray her contact didn't break protocol in a fit of worry and try to call her back.

"I hope this isn't some elaborate ploy to abduct me," he said as he opened the passenger door.

She rolled her eyes, but caught the dropped phone under the heel of her shoe and subtly pushed it under the seat. "You walk in there and you'll wish you'd been abducted," she replied, hooking a thumb at the entrance to the hotel.

"Why?"

"The jackals have found her," she replied grimly. "Frankly, I'm surprised the press has left her alone until now." Then she turned to face him, eyes narrowing. "You wouldn't have been attempting to speak to my client without me present, would you?"

He pressed a hand to his chest as if she'd wounded him with the suggestion. "Me? No. Wow. Where's the trust? I thought we had a better relationship," he said, his tone light.

She didn't let off the gas. "Then what are you doing here?"

"I came looking for you. I called your office and they said you were out at a client meeting. I used my pow-

erful deductive reasoning skills to figure out which of
your clients might need on-site consultation and here
we are." He paused, his expression becoming serious.
"I'm sorry. I shouldn't be joking about this. How is she
holding up?"

Michelle sat back, eying him skeptically as she
weighed how much truth she'd include in her answer.
"I think shock and reality are battling it out for her."

He nodded. "Understandable."

"She's trying to make arrangements, but she can't
do much yet."

Ethan drummed his fingers on his leg. She realized
he was uncomfortable. She waited, looking for other
tells as the silence stretched taut between them. He'd
said he had come there looking for her. He would have
to be the one to initiate the conversation.

"Mr. Dennis and Mrs. Cantrell both seem to be under
the impression your client did this."

"And what would be her motive?"

He shrugged. "Pick one."

She held his gaze. "They don't know the will has
been changed."

"Which will no doubt add fuel to their fire." He
propped his elbow on the door and turned to rub his
forehead. "Good call beating them to the punch by telling us."

"As my client has told you, she has nothing to hide."

He fixed those probing gray eyes on her again. "She
hid the existence of a new will."

"From people who have a vested interest in the law
firm, not from the police."

"I understand the reasoning, but either way this new
will is not going to play well for your client."

"You let me worry about how to handle my client," she snapped. When he blinked in surprise, she took her tone down a notch. "I'm sorry. I know you didn't have to come here. I am all too aware we could, and probably should, be taking a far more adversarial approach to all this." She gestured to the hotel parking lot. "This isn't the best place for detailed explanations, but let me apologize for snapping at you. I've had a number of people try to tell me how I should be doing my job today, and it's put me on the defensive."

Ethan had the grace to let her off the hook. "Which is understandable for a defense attorney." He glanced over his shoulder at the hotel entrance. "And you are correct. I shouldn't have approached you in the parking lot…or climbed into your car," he added with a rueful smile.

She chuckled, then gave her head a slow shake. "You want me to pull out of here and drop you off on the other side of the hotel." It was a joke, of course, but to her shock, Ethan seemed to be giving the plan real consideration.

"Actually, it probably couldn't hurt."

She stared at him dumbfounded as he twisted in the passenger seat, surveilling the parking area. "Are you serious?"

"How would it go over with your boss if someone told him they'd seen me get out of your car in front of the hotel where Mrs. Powers is currently in residence?"

"Not well," she conceded.

"Take your 'not well' and multiply it by ten and you'd have my captain's reaction."

"Then why did you get in the car?" she asked, curious.

On the surface Ethan Scott came across as straitlaced as any state police investigator, but there was something off about him. He didn't seem to approach his investigation with the linear kind of reasoning one usually found in cops. He seemed more like a guy who liked to find angles. The type to play devil's advocate.

"Because you told me to." When she fixed him with a bland stare, he shrugged. "I was curious."

"About?"

"You," he responded without missing a beat.

"Me?" she asked, instantly wary.

"I can't quite figure out how you fit into the PP&W puzzle," he said, glancing back again. "Probably not a bad idea to drive out of here."

Michelle checked her mirror and saw one of the reporters had come outside to smoke. "Yeah. Okay." She waited until she'd backed out and made a right turn onto the street before pressing again. "What do you mean how I fit in?"

Ethan's head swiveled when she passed the street that would take them to the rear of the hotel. "Is this turning into an abduction?"

"It's a conversation. Your turn to answer my question," she prompted, slowing for a traffic light.

"As you know, I met with Harold Dennis, Delray and William Powers and Natalie Cantrell today."

She nodded. "Yes, and…?"

"They didn't mention you."

She wasn't surprised to hear it, but she forced herself to lift her eyebrows. "Mention me in what context?"

"Any? All?" he replied. "They had a lot to say about Tyrone and Trey, of course, and much of the discussion revolved around Kayla Powers. But they never mentioned you, and that struck me as odd."

Michelle considered her response. Obviously, he was working his way around to something. Leading her somewhere. Almost as if she was a witness. "Why, do you think?"

He gave her a half smile, then nodded to the light to indicate it had turned green. "Since you've abducted me, I'm going to need to be fed. Can we go through a drive-through? I'm starved."

She nodded to a fast-food outlet ahead. "Will this work?"

"Perfect." When she made the turn into the drive-through lane, he pivoted in his seat to look directly at her. "You are an associate of their firm representing the woman they all believe to be capable of committing a double homicide. One which happened to include a man you were representing until the day he died." He hummed softly, then shook his head. "Seems to me your name would have come up at least once. The omission was glaringly obvious."

"Perhaps they don't see my counsel as a threat," she hazarded as they moved forward in line.

"Yet you were good enough for them to hire away from your East Coast firm. Good enough to handle the defense for the heir apparent," he pointed out.

"Honestly, I don't think anyone expected me to get Trey Powers out of his mess unscathed. They were all about distancing the firm from the Murray case and minimizing the impact his trial might have on their reputation. He was removed from the list of junior partners and his photo deleted from the website."

He remained quiet. As the seconds ticked by, a shiver ran up her spine. The car ahead of them moved and she let off the brake enough to roll up to the menu. "What'll it be?"

"Number one combo. Sweet tea to drink," he replied, without even glancing at the board.

She placed his order, then added an unsweetened tea for herself. His mouth kicked up in a half smile as he pulled his wallet out of his hip pocket. "You're definitely not from 'round here."

"Because I don't want a half gallon of corn syrup added to my drink?"

He nodded, his expression sobering. "Unsweet tea, the accent, the absence of excessive use of polite address—"

"Lack of what? I'm polite," she retorted, affronted.

"Gratuitous use of *sir* and *ma'am*," he clarified as he handed her a crisp bill to cover their tab.

"Oh, let me." She started to reach for her bag, but he waved her away.

"I can cover your Yankee tea."

"Yankee tea," she muttered as she rolled up to the window and thrust his money at the young woman hanging halfway out. She settled their drinks into the cup holders, then passed the bag to him. Before pulling away, she beamed a sunny smile at the restaurant employee. "Thank you, ma'am," she said in an exaggerated drawl. "Y'all have a great day now, hear?"

Ethan let out a startled bark of laughter as she pulled away. "Please don't do the drawl—it's horrible," he chortled.

"My accent is dead-on," she insisted.

"Your attempt at an accent is dead wrong."

Michelle couldn't help but smile as she checked to pull into traffic again. "Make sure you get the right drink," she instructed as he unwrapped a straw and jabbed it into a lid.

"Don't worry, I'm not drinking your brown iced water," he assured her.

He pulled the container of fries from the bag and offered it to her. She waved the fries away with a brisk, "No, thanks," though her mouth watered as the scent filled the car. She'd make sweet potato fries with her dinner, she decided there and then. "Okay, well, abduction's over," she said as she took the first right turn and headed back in the direction of the hotel.

Ethan had extracted his cheeseburger from the bag and was unwrapping it with undue care. "Who are you really?"

He asked the question in such a conversational manner she almost answered truthfully, to see if he'd believe her. But she'd impulsiveness trained out of her by the Bureau long ago. "What? Do you think I'd divulge my superhero alter ego without a credible threat against the galaxy?"

She slowed for a stop sign, then signaled to turn onto the street behind Kayla's hotel. Rather than responding to her pathetic attempt at a joke, he took a healthy bite out of his burger. The ticktock of her turn indicator filled the yawning silence. At last, he reached for his cup, stuck the straw in his mouth and swallowed the bite with a deep draw on the straw.

"I think you're a cop. Or you were a cop," he amended, staring down at his lunch with a scowl.

She gaped at him as he stuck a probing finger under the top bun, extracted a pickle slice and dropped it into the bag. Heat filled her chest, raced up her neck and set her ears aflame. "What? Why?" she sputtered, then, recovering a shred of her shaken composure, made the turn with her face averted. "I mean, what would make you think so?"

"I'm a cop," he answered as if the answer should have been obvious. "Like recognizes like."

"I'm an attorney," she said, adding a scoff of laughter. "Did you forget?"

"Nope." He took another bite, then chewed thoughtfully as she approached the rear of the hotel. "But I think you're also a cop. Grace Reed does, too."

He added the last part on as if it were the final nail in his argument.

"I don't know why—"

Before she could deflect even further, he pointed to a service drive leading to the lot where hotel employees parked. "Here is fine."

He closed the wrapper around his burger and dropped it back into the grease-stained bag. He was pulling his fructose-laden tea from the cup holder before she had drawn to a complete stop.

"Listen—"

"No, I get it," he interrupted. "There are things going on here I don't understand. I'm all too aware of what I don't know," he grumbled. But when he looked up, his eyes were sharp and direct. "But whatever it is, you can trust me with it."

"I don't know what makes you think there is anything," she said, waving her hand in airy dismissal of a ridiculous idea.

"My gut is rarely wrong," he announced, his expression grave. "My gut and Grace's?" He shook his head. "No way you've fooled us both."

She opened her mouth to protest, but he turned away,

pulling at the door handle. "All I wanted to tell you is I see you," he said as the door swung open. "We see you," he corrected. "And we're all on the same side."

"I don't get where this is coming from," she protested, but it sounded weak to her own ears.

"Like recognizes like," he repeated as he climbed out of the car, leaving the tantalizing scent of fried potatoes in his wake.

"And because you're a cop, you think I might be, or have been one, too?" she asked, tilting over the steering wheel as she bent to peer up at him. She'd thought he might be a little unconventional in his thinking, but now she was wondering if she'd underestimated how far off the typical cop mark he fell.

Ethan shook his head. "Not because I'm a cop."

"Okay," she said, drawing the word out into multiple syllables. Tired of the cat and mouse, she asked the direct question. "You got something more than hunches in your back pocket?"

"You can trust me, Ms. Fraser," he repeated.

"So you've said. Because we're all cops," she added dryly. "Allegedly."

"Right. And because I'm a cop who is also a lawyer." He backed up a step, then turned to make his way up the service drive, fast-food bag and cup clutched in one hand. "Like recognizes like," he called over his shoulder.

Michelle stared after him, the shiver she'd felt earlier turning into a ball of ice in the pit of her stomach as she watched him walk away without looking back.

Had she been made?

Was her cover blown?

He'd met with the senior partners at PP&W. Did they

know? Did Ethan Scott know for certain, or was he bluffing to see if he could make her blink first? The same thought ran through her head on a continuous loop as she pulled away from the curb. She swung a wide left turn on the first street leading away from the hotel. Beneath the heel of her shoe, the burner phone she'd dropped earlier vibrated, but did not ring.

Her contact at the Bureau sending a message to check on her welfare no doubt. Two blocks down, she pulled over and fished the phone from under the seat. The screen read only—

What do you want for dinner?

Biting her lip, she inhaled deeply before she typed out the reply chosen to assure her contact she was alive and unharmed.

Pizza is fine.

Once the message was sent, she pressed the hand holding the phone to her hammering heart.

Chapter Nine

Ethan stared at the forensics report filling his computer screen, practically willing it to offer up a suspect, any random suspect, but no such luck. All of the fingerprint and DNA evidence collected at the crime scene could be matched to the victims or the same handful of people—Kayla Powers, Senator William Powers or Harold Dennis.

The senator and Mr. Dennis were away at the time of the murders.

He ran his hand over his mouth, pulling at his cheeks as he closed his eyes. He'd been looking at the report so long, it felt like the information was emblazoned on his eyelids. He scraped his palm over his jaw and added the rasp of the day's growth of beard to the list of things prickling him. At the top of the list stood Michelle Fraser and her cagey, but selectively forthcoming, manner. Even her presence on the list rubbed him the wrong way. He had a double homicide on his hands and zero time to be chasing hunches down rabbit holes.

He opened his eyes and clicked on the email with the grainy camera footage they'd been able to obtain from the security company for the lake house. The file had been edited to only the time frame he'd requested when he'd

submitted the request through Senator Powers's local offices, but included both interior and exterior views. He'd
asked Grace Reed to review it while he was conducting
interviews. She'd written a detailed report of all the video
footage, including time stamps for reference. She'd also
summed the whole thing up succinctly:

> "This woman was barely coherent enough to get
> to the bathroom on her own. There's no way she
> drove to Bentonville, shot two grown men and
> left the scene without leaving any additional evi-
> dence."

Ethan was only on the third of the time stamps referenced by his best investigator and already inclined to
agree. The odds of Kayla Powers rousing herself from
the drunken disarray captured on the security footage,
driving miles of winding mountain roads to commit
the crime and leaving again without anyone seeing her
or any record of her coming and going were beyond
slim. Not only was the woman stone drunk for most
of the weekend, but she also never made it past the
lake house's expansive great room with its expansive
view, priceless artwork and twenty-four-hour security.
Other than the bathroom breaks Grace Reed referenced,
Kayla Powers was within camera range nearly the entire weekend.

So if he ruled Mrs. Powers, the senator and Harold
Dennis out, he needed to come up with other options.
He drew the yellow legal pad he used to take notes
closer and tried to open his mind to the alternatives.

At the top of the list was the possibility of a hit carried out by a professional. Though such events were not

as prevalent as Hollywood would have people think, they were not unheard of. Money always talked, and dead men told no tales.

He listed Senator Powers, but drew a line through the name. Not only were there several witnesses to his presence on the congressional junket, but everyone also had video footage of a man in an airport half a world away.

Harold Dennis didn't strike Ethan as the type of man who liked mess, but first impressions were not always accurate. The private jet he and the senator had flown on had returned to Arkansas the following day, but getting his hands on flight plans on a private plane heading for an island nation would be a stretch. And, though the lawyer was giving the appearance of full cooperation, there had been holes in his alibi. Holes he didn't seem inclined to sew up tight enough for Ethan's satisfaction.

Dennis was divorced. His children were grown. He lived alone and was traveling alone. According to Ethan's interview notes, no one had met him at the airport. He had planned to stay at a private residence booked through a concierge travel service. The same company had left a car parked at the airport for his use. The car he'd left parked in the same spot from which he'd retrieved it when he boarded a commercial flight back to Arkansas. It seemed like a lot of gyrations for a man like Harold Dennis.

He then listed Kayla Powers. Like it or not, she was still the person with the opportunity and access, even if he personally felt the odds of her committing the crime were extremely low. Then again, she would have the means to hire it out.

He drew an arrow from her name to the professional, then added a question mark. He had a team working the couple's financials. He'd lean into the murder-for-hire angle. He'd also take a closer look at Natalie Cantrell.

She had seemed eager to volunteer the names of people who'd seen her in Little Rock over the course of the weekend, and she would have been a more likely suspect if Trey Powers hadn't been killed as well. He could see a woman like Natalie using some of Tyrone's own money to off her ex and put her son in the driver's seat. But no matter how brittle the ex-wife came across, her adoration of Trey was something universally acknowledged. The only way he could see her being involved was if the set-up had gone tragically wrong.

Ethan flipped through the pages of notes he'd made so far. The only persons he'd interviewed, but whose fingerprints hadn't been found at the scene, were Senator Powers's son, Delray, and Nancy Ayers, the ultra-efficient assistant Tyrone and Harold shared.

He sat back and stretched. His neck popped as he rolled it to work the knots out of it. The greasy fast-food burger he'd had earlier sat heavy in his stomach, even hours later. His conversation with Michelle continued to weigh on him as well.

He was the kind of guy who asked direct questions. He didn't like spending time wondering when questions could be asked and answered. Still, he couldn't help wondering about the mysterious Ms. Fraser. He wasn't exactly sure what kept holding him back, which made him feel off kilter.

He snatched up his phone and placed the call.

She answered on the second ring. "Detective Scott," she greeted. "Working overtime?"

"Yeah, well, the clock is ticking," he said brusquely.

His terse tone zapped the teasing note from her voice. "What can I do for you?"

"Who are you, and what are you working on?" he asked without preamble.

There was a long pause. "I thought we'd already covered this, but my name is Michelle Fraser, and I am an attorney. I represent Mrs. Kayla Powers, who found her husband and stepson dead at the marital home after returning from a weekend away."

"You're a cop."

"No, you're the cop," she replied with exaggerated patience. "I am an attorney for a firm called Powers, Powers & Walton. You have a nifty leather wallet with a badge on one side and an identification card saying you work for the Arkansas State Police. Ringing a bell yet?"

"Before you became an attorney," he persisted.

"I went to law school."

"I have your résumé," he said tersely.

"Then why are you asking me questions?"

"There's a two-year gap."

"I traveled. It's not unusual," she answered, shortening her delivery to match his.

"Grace and I think you're a cop."

There was an infinitesimal pause, but he'd swear it was there. "Wow, we've gone straight to conspiracy theories," she drawled. "Do give Special Agent Reed my best."

"What are you working on?" he pushed.

"Essentially the opposite of what you're working on," she shot back.

"No. You're trying to help us solve this, right?" he persisted.

"Because it behooves my client to do so."

"Behooves," he mocked. "Is it an alphabet agency?"

"I have no idea what you mean, but I did master the alphabet well before kindergarten."

"Do you work for an agency known by an acronym?"

"Most people call it PP&W."

He harrumphed and instantly regretted his pique because the break gave her the opening she needed to redirect his line of questioning.

"I will tell you Harold Dennis has called a meeting with all your favorite people for tomorrow morning at ten."

"Called a meeting for what purpose?"

"He said succession planning for the firm, but since both William Powers and Natalie Cantrell are present and accounted for, I would not be surprised if it includes a reading of the will he intends to submit to probate."

"And I assume you and your client plan to be in attendance to submit the more recently, uh…" He stumbled to a stop. *Executed* was the only word coming to mind, but in light of the manner in which the victims had been killed, he hesitated to use it. "The will Mr. and Mrs. Powers had drawn up in Little Rock," he concluded.

"Precisely."

"And you anticipate trouble," he surmised.

"I don't think any of them will be excited by the change, no." She gave a short laugh. "I don't expect a fistfight, but I also didn't expect to be drawn into the middle of a double homicide investigation."

Unable to resist, he tried one last time to get a straight answer out of her, "What did you expect to be working on?"

A beat passed before she replied, "Trey Powers's defense, of course."

"Of course." He sighed and squeezed the back of his neck to release some of the tension gathered at the base of his skull.

"Anyhow, since you called, I thought I'd let you know."

"Did you know your client drank herself blind drunk while she was up at the lake house over the weekend?"

"I told you she'd had some wine."

He gave a derisive snort. "Your definition of *some* and mine differ by about three bottles."

"What's your point?"

He sighed and sat back, his shoulders slumping.

"No point. I can tell you I've clocked your client at about 99.5 percent innocent."

"What's holding you back on the other 0.5 percent?"

"Oh, you know, the usual… Pesky things like motive, opportunity, proximity, access…"

"She wasn't the only one with all of those things."

"But she was the only one who claims to have been alone for the entire weekend."

"Right, but now you have video evidence of where she was and what she was doing."

"Maybe she has a look-alike stashed somewhere, and she set up this whole elaborate scheme to cover her tracks. Isn't that how it usually goes on TV? How do I know she doesn't have an evil twin?"

"You're tired. Call it a day," she suggested, her voice gentle.

"Don't be nice to me now," he ordered gruffly.

"I've been nice to you all along," she chided. "I'm a nice person."

"You're a cop," he murmured. "I feel it in my bones. I read it in every move you make. Who are you, and what are you doing here?"

"I think we've talked enough for one day," she said softly.

"Michelle—"

"Ethan—"

"You can tell me. You can trust me." When she didn't respond or immediately dismiss his offer, hope flamed in the pit of his stomach. "Maybe I can help."

"You can't help me. You have enough on your plate," she reminded him. "Don't worry about me and what I have going on."

"I can't help it. I need to know."

"No, you don't," she replied in a matter-of-fact tone. "It's absolutely none of your business."

"If it's tied to this investigation—"

"I can assure you it's not."

"But there is something," he said, sitting up straight in the chair as they both realized he'd boxed her in. When she didn't speak, he pulled the phone away from his ear to make sure the call was still connected. Three seconds ticked by before she spoke again.

"Keep your eyes on your own paper, Lieutenant Scott."

"Maybe we can help each other," he insisted.

"You can help me by figuring out who actually did this. It was not Kayla Powers."

"Are you looking into something connected to the firm?"

"Good night, Ethan," she said abruptly.

"Michelle, wait—"

But it was too late. She'd ended the call. Without

giving himself a chance to think about it, he redialed. This time when she answered, she sounded frustrated and edgy.

"I have nothing more to say, Lieutenant Scott. I can't state it any more clearly. Unless you have reason to call me concerning my client, leave me alone."

"I'm sorry, but I—"

"We are not birds of the feather. We're not team players." She bit off each short sentence, her tone clipped and final. "You have your mission here, and I have mine. And if, by chance, they were to ever intersect, I wouldn't need to come to you for help."

She ended the call again, and this time Ethan did not try to call back. Instead, he lowered his phone and pushed away from the modular workstation wedged into the corner of his hotel room.

Michelle Fraser was doing something more than practicing law. She was more than another attorney on the PP&W roster.

Grace's instincts had not been wrong. Neither were his.

Michelle Fraser was a cop, but the knowledge was no comfort to him. Rather than feeling validated by the knowledge, he felt a tremor of fear pass through him.

Clearly, whatever she was doing, she was operating alone. Undercover? Most likely. Her résumé had been impeccable and airtight. Those two years easily explained away with travel. He knew plenty of lawyers who'd gone off on one last adventure before settling in for the long slog toward partnership. But she was wrong. They were alike in more ways than she'd ever know.

She was a cop masquerading as a lawyer, and he was a lawyer who found his calling in being a cop.

THE FOLLOWING MORNING, fueled by a sausage, egg and cheese croissant and an extralarge coffee from the local doughnut shop, Ethan settled in at his borrowed desk in the Benton County Correctional Complex and began making phone calls. The first he placed was to Grace Reed.

"C.I.D. Agent Reed speaking," she said briskly.

He chuckled at her formal greeting. "Don't you ever check your caller ID?"

"Always."

"You answer every call so formally? Even if it's your sister?" he challenged.

"Especially if it's my sister," she replied without rancor. "Can't have her forgetting which one of us is the badass."

"Absolutely not," he agreed.

"What's up, Chief?"

"I got a half-baked admission out of Michelle Fraser yesterday."

"Admission of what?"

Aware he was treading into unknown territory, and that someone with even a tenuous connection to the Powers family might be listening, he kept his messaging cryptic. "She may be something more than she appears."

"More than a smart, savvy attorney paid handsomely to defend the sleazebag kids of people with far too much money?"

"Exactly."

"Hmm. How half-baked was the admission?"

"On the doughy side. I asked if she liked alphabet soup, and she told me she was too busy with her current mission to enjoy it."

He heard the tap-tap-tap of Grace's pen as she parsed his meaning. "Interesting. A real workaholic, huh?"

"Might have been a habit she picked up after law school. You know, in those two years she was traveling abroad."

"Oh, traveling abroad," Agent Reed repeated with exaggerated nonchalance. "No doubt."

"You know some employers like to be sure their new hires are well traveled and well trained."

"True."

"Maybe see if she started her journey in DC or Virginia?"

He didn't need to explain to Grace that DC might mean connections to the FBI or ATF, but Virginia would likely point to a background with the CIA or DEA.

"I'll poke around and see what I can find." He could hear a pen scratching on paper as she made notes. "Anything else I can do for you?"

"Yeah. Harold Dennis. Can you collect all you have on him and forward it on to me?"

"Mr. Dennis?" Grace was clearly surprised by the request. "Sure, but wasn't he out of the country over the weekend?"

"Yes. Something else I need to follow up on. He and the senator flew out on a private jet owned by a company called DevCo. D-e-v-c-o," he spelled. "They're a client, and they let the senator and Mr. Dennis have the use of their jet. Can you or Thompson reach out to see what we can do to check flight plans, confirm passengers onboard, whatever we can get?"

"Will do," she said in her usual brisk tone.

Ethan was relieved to hear it. Their initial conversations about the case had been stilted, but as they got deeper into it and Grace realized he'd be coming to her as a resource, she seemed to relax. He couldn't blame her. She'd done an incredible job investigating Trey Powers and the circumstances surrounding Mallory Murray's death, then had the rug pulled out from under her. He would have hated handing over his files to any other investigator as well.

Feeling they were on firmer footing, he took a chance on teasing her. "Wanna trade places with me?"

"Um, no. That's a negative," she replied, but he heard the smile creep into her tone. "I'm happy to stay in the bullpen this inning, Chief."

"I'll touch base with you later," he said, then ended the call.

Before he could put the phone down, it rang in his hand. He checked the screen, grimacing when he saw Captain Will Hopkins's name. "Scott here," he answered, instinctively reaching for his pen.

"Ethan," his boss said briskly. "How are things going?"

A dozen disparaging answers sprang to mind, but Ethan squelched the urge to reply with any of them. "Things are slow to develop. Did you receive my progress report?"

"I did, but it didn't contain as much actual progress as I'd hoped," he responded, his tone dry as dust.

"There hasn't been as much as I'd like either, sir."

"Tell me about the widow," Hopkins ordered.

Ethan knew the boss was asking for something more than he'd put in his initial report. The head of Company D was a big believer in instinct, and thankfully, he seemed to trust Ethan's. As succinctly as possible, Ethan gave him the rundown on Kayla Powers's background, the few opinions he'd collected about her time at PP&W, general impressions he'd gathered about the couple's marriage, and then rounded it out by reminding his superior that Mrs. Powers had not only been fully cooperative, but also essentially exonerated by the video footage supplied by the security company. "All in all, sir, she's only a person of interest due to a lack of alternatives."

"Yes, I'm with you," the head of the division responded. "Who else is on your short list?"

Ethan stifled the urge to laugh at the terminology. His list was so short, it came down to only one person without an airtight alibi. Still, he had to give the boss something. "Well, I'm left with Senator Powers's son Delray, Mr. Powers's ex-wife, Natalie Cantrell, and Harold Dennis at the moment." He paused for a breath. "Truthfully, I can't see any of them pulling the trigger, though."

"You think we have a murder-for-hire situation?"

"It's possible," Ethan hedged. "No forced entry, no robbery or even the attempt to make it look like one."

"Plenty of people with money," Captain Hopkins chimed in.

"Yes, but not the bottomless pockets Tyrone Powers had," Ethan said musingly. "They're reading a will this morning."

"So soon? Have the bodies even been released?"

"No, sir, but I gather there are some questions as to the future of the firm, not to mention Tyrone Powers's personal estate—particularly since his only child is dead."

"Right," Will Hopkins said thoughtfully, drawing the word out. "Well, maybe the disposition of his assets will shed some light on who stands to benefit most."

Ethan knew who the winner of that particular lottery would be, but he did not say anything about the will Michelle Fraser had alerted him to. He wanted to wait to see how the morning's proceedings actually played out before passing the possibility of a probate war up his chain of command.

"Yes, sir. Hopefully, this family meeting will be what we need to get to the truth."

"Keep me informed, Scott," the older man ordered.

"I will, sir." With that, he pulled the phone away from his ear and checked to be sure his superior had ended the call before blowing out a gusty breath. Checking the time, he saw it was nearly the appointed hour. A quick glance at his notifications showed a new message from Michelle Fraser had arrived.

Heading in to the office. Any chance you might "coincidentally" swing by for another round of interviews while this is happening? I've got a feeling this might go sideways.

Without thinking twice, Ethan grabbed his keys and ID from the desk drawer and rose. The message gave him the impetus he needed to follow his gut. He was one step out the door when Sheriff Stenton called out to him.

"I'm on my way out," he answered, hooking a thumb toward the door.

"Walking and talking," the sheriff replied, not breaking stride. "Did you hear they're reading Tyrone Powers's will today?"

The sheriff puffed a little as they fell into step, but he didn't slow.

"I did. How did you?"

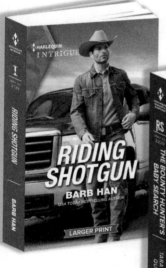

Get up to 4
FREE FABULOUS BOOKS
You Love!

To thank you for being a loyal reader we'd like to send you up to 4 FREE BOOKS, absolutely free when you try the Harlequin Reader Service.

Just write "YES" on the Loyal Reader Voucher and we'll send you 2 free books from each series you choose and a Free Mystery Gift, altogether worth over $20.

Try **Harlequin® Romantic Suspense** and get 2 books featuring heart-racing page-turners with unexpected plot twists and irresistible chemistry that will keep you guessing to the very end.

Try **Harlequin Intrigue® Larger-Print** and get 2 books featuring action-packed stories that will keep you on the edge of your seat. Solve the crime and deliver justice at all costs

Or **TRY BOTH and get 2 books from each series!**

Your free books are completely free, even the shipping! If you continue with your subscription, you can look forward to curated monthly shipments of brand-new books from your selected series, always at a discount off the cover price! Plus you can cancel any time.

So don't miss out, return your Loyal Readers Voucher today to get your Free books.

Pam Powers

LOYAL READER
FREE BOOKS VOUCHER

▶ DETACH AND MAIL CARD TODAY! ▶

YES! I Love Reading, please send me up to 4 FREE BOOKS and a Free Mystery Gift from the series I select.

Just write in "YES" on the dotted line below then return this card today and we'll send your free books & gift asap!

➡ YES ⬅

Which do you prefer?

☐ **Harlequin® Romantic Suspense**
240/340 HDL GRRX

☐ **Harlequin Intrigue® Larger-Print**
199/399 HDL GRRX

☐ **BOTH**
240/340 & 199/399
HDL GRSM

FIRST NAME	LAST NAME

ADDRESS

APT.#	CITY

STATE/PROV.	ZIP/POSTAL CODE

EMAIL ☐ Please check this box if you would like to receive newsletters and promotional emails from Harlequin Enterprises ULC and its affiliates. You can unsubscribe anytime.

HI/HRS-622-LR_MMM22

The older man huffed a laugh. "Don't let the population explosion fool you. This is still a small town."

"I guess so."

"Seems a little fast to be readin' a will," Stenton observed.

Ethan nodded. "Sounds to me like a few people have a lot at stake. I was heading over there to interview some of Trey Powers's, uh, colleagues," he said, recalling the list of close associates Grace had included in her background information.

The sheriff nodded. "A good idea. Mind if I ride along?"

Ethan glanced at the man beside him and spotted the same tension in the sheriff's jaw as he felt coiling in his own belly. The sheriff's bells were ringing, too. And though he'd long grown accustomed to working on his own, for once Ethan was glad he wasn't the only one whose cop radar was pinging.

And the knowledge he, Sheriff Stenton and Michelle Fraser were all on the same page only confirmed his hunch. Whether she'd admit it or not, the woman had cop blood pulsing through her veins.

He hit the crash bar on the exit door and held it open for the sheriff. The older man shot him a wary look. "I have a feeling today is going to be a doozy."

Ethan nodded as he jogged two steps to catch up again. "And I have a feeling you're right, Sheriff."

Chapter Ten

Michelle picked Kayla up at the hotel the following morning and delivered her directly to the front door of PP&W. As they walked through the offices, staff and associates greeted her with polite solemnity, but not with an excess of warmth. Michelle cast a sidelong glance at her client as they started up the staircase. Kayla's slender hand trembled on the rail.

"Are you okay?"

Kayla nodded, but her response was a whispered, "Of course not."

"What can I do?"

"Nothing." Her client's smile was tremulous as they proceeded up the staircase at an unrushed pace. "I...I laid off the wine last night."

"You did?"

"And now I'm thinking I could have used the fortification."

"I don't see how a hangover would help."

"It would be a distraction," Kayla said grimly. "But I thought I'd better be clearheaded for this morning."

"Smart thinking. You're going to need all your wits about you in the next few days." Michelle gave a soft chuckle as she caught Kayla's wry glance. "Okay, probably weeks," she amended. "We only need you to hold it together for now. Then you can fall apart. Or, if you want or need help when this is all over, we'll tackle whatever issues you need to deal with when the smoke has cleared."

Her gaze fixed on the top of the stairs, Kayla nodded. "My thinking exactly."

They reached the second floor, and Nancy hurried over from her desk to greet them, her arms outstretched. Michelle couldn't help noticing it was the exact same way she'd greeted Natalie Cantrell the day before. She hung back, feeling the weight of the packet of paperwork sent from Little Rock in her tote bag. To her surprise, Kayla not only accepted the older woman's motherly embrace, but also seemed to melt into Nancy's arms. Unlike Natalie Cantrell, who'd held herself stiff and apart in the scene Michelle had witnessed the day before.

As she watched Kayla extricate herself, it occurred to Michelle she hadn't offered her client much in the way of consolation. Where to draw the line was one of the tricky parts of her job. Her actual job. Life undercover often meant she was immersed in a particular world for years of her life, but the nature of what she did made close relationships impossible.

"Good morning, Nancy," she said as the older woman relinquished her hold on Kayla. "Harold asked us to come in to speak with him about some firm business."

Mrs. Ayers's perfectly coiffed hair bobbed as she gestured to the large conference room that took up much of the wall opposite the staircase. "Oh, yes," she said in a rush, "please come on in. Everybody is waiting," she added, then winced.

"Everybody?" Kayla asked in a tone so innocent

she might as well have been cast in the role of cartoon princess.

"I mean—" Nancy started to stammer.

"I'm sure Harold has asked William and Del to be here as well," Michelle said, cutting in smoothly.

"Oh. Of course," Kayla said, sounding mildly befuddled by the notion of the other partners of the firm assembling.

Nancy led the way to the conference room door, then paused with her hand on the nickel-plated handle. "The coffee service is set up, and there's water on the table. I've had some breakfast rolls brought in. If you need anything at all, y'all let me know."

"We will," Michelle responded. "Thank you."

Kayla flashed another shaky smile. "Yes. Thank you, Nancy."

"Of course, sugar. Anything you need. Anything at all, you let me know."

The older woman pushed the door open and announced them. "Mrs. Powers and Ms. Fraser are here," she said briskly.

Michelle stepped into the room behind her client. To her credit, Kayla didn't shrink back at the sight of Natalie Cantrell seated at the long mahogany table. Senator Powers, a younger, more ruthlessly preserved version of his older brother, stood at their entrance. His son and Harold Dennis hastened to follow suit.

"Oh, don't get up on our account," Kayla said, trying to wave them into their seats.

But William Powers was already on the move. With his gaze locked on his sister-in-law, he circled the end of the long table and came to stand in front of Kayla, his arms outstretched for an embrace.

Kayla hesitated only for a moment before stepping into the hug. "I'm so sorry," she whispered, her voice breaking on the sentiment.

"I think I'm supposed to be consoling you," the senator replied in a voice rough with emotion.

Michelle hung back, observing their interaction with the detached interest of a person watching a stage performance. Senator William Powers, urbane and polished to a high sheen despite the horrid circumstances, appeared to be every inch the grieving sibling hoping to console his distraught sister-in-law.

A woman he barely stopped shy of calling a murderess on a cable news network.

Michelle couldn't help wondering what he truly thought of his brother's marriage to someone nearly a quarter century his junior.

She took another step back as both Harold and Del approached Kayla. One by one, they exchanged brief embraces and air kisses. Words were murmured on both sides, but it was hard to gauge the level of sincerity.

Only Natalie Cantrell remained true to form.

Seated at one of the high-backed leather chairs, she pivoted enough to watch the proceedings, but didn't bother to rise from the chair. Nor did she voice any platitudes. Michelle couldn't help but admire the woman for her ability to stay true to herself at a time when most others rushed to put their best foot forward.

The men filed back to their chairs, and Kayla made eye contact with Tyrone's previous wife. To Michelle's surprise, Kayla inclined her head in the direction of the still-seated woman. "My condolences," she said, her voice husky and raw.

Natalie Cantrell looked momentarily taken aback,

but was quick to recover. "My condolences to you as well," she replied, but her words came out clipped and insincere.

Michelle directed Kayla to the chairs Hal Dennis had pulled out for them on the opposite side of the table from Tyrone's brother, nephew and ex-wife. It was clear to see the battle lines were drawn.

Harold cleared his throat. "I know this seems distastefully soon to be discussing, but I feel it's in everybody's best interests if we make sure the firm stays on stable footing as we navigate our way through this difficult time," he began.

Michelle sat back in her chair, fighting the urge to smile as she realized he sounded like a Hollywood depiction of a southern gentleman lawyer.

"There's already been some speculation, and I have to admit, jockeying," he added, his tone dripping with disdain, "among the associates."

"Let me guess. Chet Barrow thinks he should be the next in line for junior partnership, since he was the closest to Trey," Michelle said dryly.

"Chet Barrow is a fine young man from an excellent family," Natalie said, leaping to the ambitious young lawyer's defense.

Harold silenced them both with a stern glare. "I won't name any names because everybody is operating under strain these days. Nor will I tolerate anyone casting aspersions on other people's ambitions. Having ambition is a positive attribute in our line of work, not a detriment. Either way, I prefer to give people the benefit of the doubt. Stressful situations don't always allow individuals to show their best colors."

Michelle shot Kayla a glance but the younger woman

sat still. Frozen. Obviously waiting on pins and needles for the real fireworks to start.

"But discussions such as this are why I think it's important to establish at least a temporary hierarchy within the firm. Therefore, for the foreseeable future, I will be acting as managing partner until such time as Delray feels comfortable in taking over the role," he said, nodding deferentially to both the senator and his son.

Michelle zoomed in on Del. The young man's face showed nothing more than solemn acceptance of the new role thrust upon him. Or was it resignation?

"We appreciate your willingness to step into the breach," Senator Powers said, his sonorous voice echoing in the large conference room. "I know Del here—" At this point he clapped a hand onto his son's shoulder. Michelle didn't miss Del's surprised reaction. "Well, he's a fast learner, and I believe he'll pick up the mantle of leadership quickly. We'd hate to place an undue burden on you for any extended period of time, Hal. I know you've had an eye on retiring soon."

"It's no trouble," Harold Dennis said graciously. He opened the leather dossier in front of him and placed his palms flat on the surface of the gleaming table. "As a matter of fact, I'm only following the directives given to me by Tyrone himself when we drew up his last will and testament."

"Excuse me," Michelle interrupted. "Can you tell us when the will you're referencing was executed?"

Harold seemed taken aback by the question. "The date?" He shook his head in bewilderment, then flipped to the last page in the file. "This will was signed and witnessed on six years ago, when Trey joined the firm. Why?"

"Witnessed by?" Michelle prompted.

"Myself, and Nancy Ayers," he answered in a clipped tone. "Again, why do you ask?"

At this point Michelle pulled the heavy manila envelope from her tote bag. The seal was intact, and the address embossed on the upper left-hand corner showed it to be from Anderson & Associates in Little Rock.

"I ask because I believe you are referring to an outdated will," she stated calmly.

"What? How can that be?" Natalie Cantrell demanded, her head swiveling as she switched her glare from Michelle to Harold, then back again.

"Mr. and Mrs. Powers had new documents drawn up after they were married." She offered Natalie Cantrell a small, tight smile. "As one would expect after a divorce, of course."

Across the table William Powers assented with a soft, "Of course," though his jaw clenched tight.

Del looked confused, and Natalie visibly upset.

"I have no knowledge of such a document," Harold Dennis said stiffly. "I've been handling Tyrone's personal business for nearly thirty years, and he's never said a word to me about changing his will after he and Natalie separated."

Michelle slid the sealed envelope across the glossy table. It came to a stop short of Harold Dennis's leather portfolio. "Mr. and Mrs. Powers opted to engage outside counsel for the purposes of revising their instructions. Anderson & Associates in Little Rock."

Harold Dennis looked down at the envelope. The corner of his upper lip twitched up when he read the name of the small, boutique firm, but he caught the sneer before it could take hold. "I've never heard of this firm," he said in a tone so officious it could almost make one believe if he hadn't personally approved the creation of the other firm, it couldn't exist on this earthly plane.

"One of my friends from law school is a partner there," Kayla said, speaking up for the first time since they'd been seated. "Tyrone wanted to use somebody from outside of the PP&W family. He wanted his wishes to be captured by someone wholly without bias or a stake in the firm."

If she had chosen her words to be incendiary, she hit the mark. Almost immediately Harold, William, Natalie and Del started sputtering and spouting their indignation. Michelle let them go for a moment before raising her hand in a call for silence.

"If you'd like, you can go ahead and read the document you prepared six years ago—you are more than welcome to—but I think you'll see these new papers are much more recent." She turned to Kayla. "When did you sign the new documents?"

"April of last year," she answered without hesitation.

"This is highly irregular," Harold protested.

Michelle cocked her head and wrinkled her brow as she studied the older man. "Is it? Seems to me as family counsel you should have suggested he rewrite portions of his will when his first marriage ended."

"Yes, well, yes. He should have come to me to make the changes."

She shook her head. "But he isn't required to. I know a number of attorneys who use counsel from outside their own firms to draw up legal documents. It saves a lot of hassle in the event those documents are later disputed."

"What are the terms of this new will?" Natalie Cantrell demanded.

Kayla opened her mouth to speak, but Michelle quieted her with a gentle hand pressed on her arm. "Mr. Dennis has the documents. Let's let him read them aloud now so there can be no question as to how your late husband wished to proceed from here."

The four people seated across the table stared at her, frozen by shock and displeasure. At last, Harold Dennis snatched up the envelope, stuck his index finger under the flap and ripped it open.

The thick sheaf of papers inside indicated Tyrone had indeed spelled out his wishes in great detail. But given what Kayla had told her about the terms of the will, most of those details would be lost to posterity, since Trey was deceased as well.

"I, Tyrone Delray Powers, Junior..." Dennis began, his eyes scanning far ahead as his words trailed off.

Natalie Cantrell leaned in. "Well? What does it say?"

Harold held up a finger to stay her questioning as his eyes moved faster and faster across the pages. "Trey would have remained primary." He flipped one sheet over, shaking his head as he read onto the second page of the document. "I don't—" he muttered as he continued to read.

"What?" Senator Powers demanded, all overblown civility gone.

"She gets it," Harold said more clearly, shaking his head and reading as quickly as he could. "She gets it all," he said, his voice rising in disbelief.

He flipped another page and Michelle craned her

neck to see if he'd reached the signatory statements and the notary's declaration about entity. Ignoring the detailed addendum stacked below those all-important first pages, he flipped back to the beginning.

"Damn it, Harold, what do you mean?" Natalie Cantrell demanded.

Harold finally looked up and met the other woman's gaze. "He left it all to Trey, of course, but then in the event Trey predeceased him or died before the will could be processed through probate, he has left everything to his...wife." He spoke the last word with such raw bitterness Michelle felt Kayla flinch beside her. "Kayla Powers is to take over as managing partner of PP&W effective immediately."

Natalie slapped a hand on the table. "We'll contest it," she said without hesitation.

"On what grounds?" Michelle demanded. "You and Mr. Powers are long divorced. As a matter of fact, you remarried within months of the paperwork being filed. Your son has, unfortunately, died before Tyrone's will could go through probate. You have no material interest here."

"She coerced him," Natalie accused.

"Prove it," Michelle challenged, keeping a quelling hand on her client's arm. "No judge is going to overturn a properly witnessed will favoring a current spouse in favor of an ex. I believe, under the circumstances, it could be argued Mr. Dennis was negligent in not ensuring Mr. Powers amend his will prior to last year." She fixed her gaze on Natalie Cantrell. "Truthfully, I'm not sure why you are here."

"It's none of your business why I am here," Natalie snapped back.

"Actually, it is," Michelle responded coolly.

"Who are you, anyway?" Natalie swiveled toward Harold, then William. "Isn't she an employee of this firm? She should be fired for such…"

When she paused, grasping for a word, Michelle couldn't help providing her own answer. "Truth telling?"

"Insubordination," the other woman spat out.

"Ah, but I would have to fire her, and I don't want to," Kayla said, her tone calm and firm.

"Now, Natalie," Harold said in a patently consoling tone.

"You told me I was named in Ty's will as a beneficiary," she blurted.

"Ty's outdated will," Kayla murmured under her breath.

"Of course, Tyrone had every right to draw up a new will after the divorce was finalized," William said, smoothly inserting himself into the confrontation. "But by 'everything' you can't mean all of Tyrone's assets, both business and personal," he said with such an air of jocular disbelief one was almost tempted to chuckle along with him.

"I mean all of it," Harold said. He flipped the document back to the first page and picked it up and practically tossed it into the senator's lap. "He has left his interest in the firm, the entirety of his personal estate, as well as his share of the family trust and all of its holdings, to Kayla Powers."

"My, my, what an advantageous marriage you've made," Natalie Cantrell drawled.

Kayla shook her head. "It was never supposed to come to me. Trey was the intended heir. You can see by the attached codicils I was only ever supposed to get the spousal portion of any assets accrued since our marriage. There's a will in there for me as well, which stipulates any interest in the firm and family assets were to revert to the family trust if we had no children of our own to inherit."

"Which you do not," Natalie said with a sneer.

"We do not," Kayla confirmed, her voice soft. But she sat up straighter in her chair and looked the older woman straight in the eye. "But you could not honestly believe I was going to allow him to leave you in place as the secondary beneficiary."

Kayla turned to Harold, effectively dismissing her predecessor.

"And you as the family attorney should have advised Tyrone to amend his will long ago. You didn't, and your lack of oversight was one of the reasons he chose to retain outside counsel. Ty wasn't entirely certain you had his best interests at heart."

"Now, you listen here," Harold Dennis said, rising from his seat.

"How do we know this isn't something you drew up yourself?" William asked, the razor-sharp implication of the question slicing through the tension in the room.

Kayla turned to stare at the man who'd embraced her so warmly mere minutes earlier. "Excuse me?"

William Powers looked up, his gaze appraising as he seemed to take his sister-in-law's measure for the first time. "How do we know you didn't fabricate this document?" He shrugged. "It seems convenient you happen to have a copy of a will nobody else has heard of on hand. One my brother didn't even discuss with me, much less with the family attorney," he said, nodding to Hal. "It seems oddly convenient."

Kayla gaped at him. "Convenient?"

"Perhaps a poor word choice," said the senator with a conciliatory gesture, but the sentiment rang insincere. The man was a career politician; words were his bread and butter. "Coincidental?"

"What are you saying?" Michelle asked, raising one eyebrow.

"I'm saying there's no proof this will is not a forgery," he replied, as easily as if stating the time of day.

"There's a copy of it in the safe in Tyrone's office," Kayla said firmly.

"How do we know you didn't place it there after Ty was killed?" Senator Powers shot back.

"Because I haven't been in this building for months. Check your security footage. Check the hotel's footage. Every minute of my life has been accounted for since I came home and found my husband and his son brutally murdered in my home," she retorted, her voice quaking with rage.

"Who all has the combination to the safe?" Michelle asked, though she already knew the answer.

"Tyrone, and I believe Trey," Kayla replied.

"Do you?" Michelle asked.

She shook her head. "No, but he did tell me where he kept a list of his passwords and such hidden."

"Would Mrs. Ayers or any other member of staff have reason to access Tyrone's office safe?" Michelle pressed, looking from one person to the next.

"The safes were for our personal use," William replied stiffly. "We were not supposed to keep firm business in there."

"But obviously, there would be some instances where those lines might be blurred," Michelle asserted. Pushing back from the table, she rose. "Shall we go look for it?" she asked her client.

Kayla nodded mutely and began to rise.

"But it would prove nothing," Natalie said as the others followed suit. "Even I know where Tyrone kept his combinations and passwords written on a piece of yellow legal pad under the pencil divider in his center drawer," she said as they filed out of the conference room.

Michelle saw the corner of Kayla's mouth kick up, and wondered if it was because her husband had indeed been a creature of habit, or if she was about to prove Tyrone's ex-wife wrong. When they reached the door to the corner office, Nancy Ayers rose from her seat, a look of puzzled concern furrowing her brows. Harold Dennis brushed past the assemblage and reached for the door handle.

"Mr. Dennis—" Nancy said as he attempted to open the door and found it locked.

He looked over at the flustered woman, annoyance written all over his face. "Why is this door locked?"

"Because I asked it be locked and kept locked while our investigation is still active," a deep male voice said from one of the adjacent seating areas.

They turned almost as one, and Michelle saw Ethan Scott and Sheriff Stenton pushing out of their seats.

The lieutenant gave her a wry smile as they approached. "The sheriff and I thought it best to secure both offices. I'm sorry. I thought Mrs. Ayers might have mentioned it."

"There wasn't, um..." The woman stammered to a

stop when Dennis glared at her. "You didn't tell me you needed to go in there."

"It's okay. You can unlock it now if you would, Nancy," the sheriff said genially. "I don't want to get you in hot water with your boss."

"We need access to Tyrone's wall safe," Harold Dennis said coolly, straightening to his full height as the lieutenant and the sheriff joined them. "On private firm business."

"It's okay," Kayla Powers said quickly. "They can come in with us."

With her head bowed, Nancy Ayers took a ring of keys from her drawer and sidled through the center of the knot to get to the door. The second they had access, the older woman shrank back so as not to be caught in the stampede. Michelle hung back to walk in with Ethan Scott.

"You're missing an interesting morning," she said in a low voice.

"I wish I'd been invited," he murmured back. "Looks like all the cool kids were."

"Okay, where is the combination?" Harold Dennis called, clearly in a hurry to get this exercise over.

Natalie Cantrell walked over to the large antique desk she'd selected to furnish the office nearly twenty years before and slid the center drawer open. But when she lifted the pencil tray, her preternaturally smooth brow puckered slightly. "Oh."

"Yeah, I told him that wasn't the best place to hide things," Kayla said, for the first time in days sounding like the bright, self-assured woman she was. "Try the bottom left drawer. There should be a file folder marked 'C. Klein Briefs.'" Michelle looked over at her sharply, but her client's smile had turned soft and misty. "He thought it was funny."

A moment later, Harold Dennis pulled out a manila folder with a neatly printed label marked exactly as Kayla had said.

"It is funny," Michelle whispered to her client, knowing she would need to bolster her through this last part.

"It's full of blank paper," Harold reported.

"One page is not blank," Kayla assured him.

The older man fanned the pages, then froze when he flicked past one with a neat column of numbers, phrases, nonsense words and other alphanumerical combinations. Without speaking, he withdrew it from the file and let the rest drop to the floor where the papers scattered at his feet. Paper crunched under the soles of his hand-tooled leather shoes as he moved to a painting of a riverbed in the autumn and swung the frame aside.

Michelle and Ethan exchanged a glance at the other lawyer's direct approach, but said nothing. They watched as the older man twirled the old-fashioned dial on the square wall safe.

Then, as the door swung open on well-oiled hinges, they all took a step forward, crowding to see into the small, dark space.

"Well, I'll be," Harold whispered, almost to himself. Michelle elbowed her way past Natalie Cantrell in time to see his hand close around a sealed envelope made of the same heavy paper stock as the one sent from Little Rock. When he drew it out into the open, she caught sight of the Anderson & Associates logo and return address.

Then a flash of something metal caught the morning

light coming through the blinds as it fell to the floor with a heavy thud.

A collective gasp rose from those assembled when they saw the handgun that lay on the floor.

Chapter Eleven

Ethan stepped up behind Michelle and leaned in to catch a glimpse of what the others were staring at, transfixed. A dull grey handgun lay on the thick Aubusson carpet, its barrel pointed directly at the feet of Kayla Powers. Michelle stared at the weapon, incredulity written all over her face. He couldn't blame her. It was as if her client had been chosen in some bizarre game of spin the bottle.

"Well, I'll be," the sheriff said under his breath.

"Nah," Ethan answered softly. "Too obvious."

Michelle lifted her head as if sensing danger, then turned to look at him. Before she could say anything, he asked, "Mrs. Powers, to your knowledge did your husband own a handgun?"

Kayla stared at the gun, her eyes wide. "Yes," she whispered at last. "Ty owned a number of guns. I know he kept a handgun at the house. He has hunting rifles, a crossbow…" She looked up, her brow puckered in confusion. "Do those count?" Then, as if she'd caught herself as soon as the words escape, shook her head. "No. Yes. Of course. He has all the usual array of hunting equipment. As I'm sure you saw when you searched the house and garage."

Sheriff Stenton nodded. "Yes, and we did catalog the gun kept in the wall safe you indicated in the master suite."

"Do you have any idea if this particular gun might have been a part of your husband's collection?" Ethan persisted.

Kayla shrugged. "He could have kept one here for all I know." She lifted her hands palm up in a gesture of futility. "I don't know why he would, but he could have."

Out of the corner of his eye Ethan saw Harold Dennis flex his knees as if to stoop down for a better look at the gun.

"Don't move," Ethan ordered in such a commanding tone the older man immediately froze in place. "I mean, you can stand up but please, everybody back away from the weapon. We don't know if it's secured."

Satisfied the assembled were following directions, Ethan stepped past Michelle and braced a foot on either side of the handgun and stared down at it. "Looks to be a semiautomatic," he called out to the sheriff, who'd worked his way past the others. Squatting down, he cocked his head. "No magazine in it. Do you have any gloves on you?"

The older man unsnapped one of the many compartments on his utility belt and extracted a pair of purple latex gloves. "Got a bag, too," he said as he handed over the gloves. He pulled out a small square of clear plastic and unfolded it to reveal a startlingly large evidence bag.

"Thank you," Ethan said as he took the proffered gloves and bag. "I'll need a pen or something to lift it." He shifted on his haunches, dropping one knee beside the weapon in order to pull on the gloves. Aware of the rapt attention from his audience, he called out, "I'd appreciate it if everyone could move to the other side of the room, but nobody leave."

"Here," Michelle Fraser said as she thrust an ornately engraved metal letter opener in his direction. He looked up at her in surprise. She hooked her thumb toward the desk. "I grabbed it off the desk."

"Thank you." He set the letter opener down next to the gun, pulled on the latex gloves and freed his phone from the case clipped to his belt. He took several photos of the gun in the position in which it had landed. He also captured the array of papers now scattered about the office floor and a surreptitious snap of the group of witnesses gathered now on the other side of the desk.

"I need to make sure it's completely disarmed," he explained as he lifted the gun, gingerly taking care not to handle the stock or the trigger. He knew as well as anyone it was incredibly difficult to lift decent fingerprints off a gun thanks to advances in anti-corrosion technology, but on the slim chance there were latent prints on this one, prints that did not belong to Tyrone Powers, he was going to do his best to preserve them if he could. Holding the weapon with the muzzle pointed down he opened the chamber and found a nine-millimeter bullet in place.

"Sheriff?"

"Yes, sir?" Stenton replied promptly.

"No magazine, but one in the chamber," he reported as he removed the bullet and did a visual check to be sure the barrel was clear. "Weapon has been disarmed."

Placing the gun gently back on the rug, Ethan took more photos of both the gun and the single bullet. When he was satisfied, he slipped the letter opener through the firing mechanism to hold the gun close enough to inspect it. "Appears to be a Glock 17. All serial numbers and markings intact," he relayed to the sheriff, who stood beside him taking notes. He slid the gun and the bullet into the evidence bag. "Mrs. Powers, we will be taking this gun into police custody for ballistics testing."

"Understood, Lieutenant," Kayla replied. "Do whatever you need to do."

"You know what you need to do. Didn't you see?" Natalie Cantrell said, sliding in closer to Senator Powers's side. "It was pointing right at her when it landed."

Ethan fought the urge to roll his eyes. "Coincidence, Mrs. Cantrell," he answered in a no-nonsense tone. Holding the bag closed in his gloved hand, he rose to his full height and turned to Harold Dennis. "Was this what you were looking for in the safe?"

The older man startled at the question. "What? No." He shook his head so hard his perfectly barbered steel gray hair almost moved. "We came to see if there was a copy of the will Mrs. Powers presented to us. She claimed there has been a copy kept in Tyrone's safe."

"I see." Ethan nodded to the envelope the older man clutched in his hand. "Is that what you were looking for?"

Harold Dennis raised his hand as if he had forgotten he'd been holding the thick envelope. Ethan could see the logo for a Little Rock firm stamped on the corner. He wanted to see how this drama was going to play out. "If Mrs. Powers already presented you with a copy, why did you need a second copy?"

"Because they believed I was presenting them with a forgery," Kayla Powers replied tartly.

At last, Michelle seemed to find her voice. "We came in here to prove the copy of the will presented by Mrs. Powers to Senator Powers and the rest of those gathered here today was indeed legitimate. They had their doubts, so we came to see the copy Mr. Powers kept in the safe here as he had told his wife he did."

"There should also be a copy in our safe at home," Kayla informed them, her voice husky. "I had the firm messenger the copy we gave to Mr. Dennis this morning."

Michelle stepped in. "There were some questions as to the validity of the document, but I believe finding its duplicate here today should put those doubts to rest."

"I'm not sure we can say so entirely," Senator Powers said gruffly.

Kayla turned to her brother-in-law. "Bill, do you want to fight me on this? You can if you want, but you know I'm going to win. And you're going to look like the man who's picking on a widow. Are those the optics you want to have coming into an election year?"

"Don't you threaten him," Harold Dennis said, bristling.

"I didn't threaten him," Kayla said with a scoff. She pivoted to face Ethan. "Lieutenant Scott, did you hear me threaten the senator?"

"No, ma'am," he replied, and looking each of the men in the eye, he shook his head slowly. "Her statement was not a threat. She was merely saying a family squabble would not look good in the public eye given the circumstances."

"Particularly when the bodies haven't even been released to have services," Michelle pointed out to them.

"Some might consider the purpose of this meeting to be unseemly, given the timing."

"Harold, Bill, please," Kayla began. "I understand this isn't what you believed would happen, but let's be honest, no one ever dreamed we'd be in this position—"

"Oh, someone dreamed," Mrs. Cantrell cut in. "Someone dreamed about exactly this outcome. Someone killed my son in hopes of this happening," she insisted, her voice growing shrill. She whirled on Ethan, her head thrown back and her throat taut with rage. "Aren't you going to do something? Anything?" she demanded. "Arrest her!"

Ethan scowled at the woman, but empathy won out over the impatience her imperious tone stirred. "At this time, we have no evidence—"

"Oh, for the love of all that's holy!" she cried, throwing her hands in the air. "Can you believe this? The woman is found covered in blood, two men dead in her own home. No sign of a break-in. Yet you have no evidence it was her. No evidence at all."

"Now, Mrs. Cantrell," Sheriff Stenton interjected, his tone thick and smooth as warm honey. "You know we can't divulge everything we know."

"You don't know a damn thing, Bud Stenton. My daddy always said you didn't have the sense God gave a goose."

Ethan stared wide-eyed as Natalie Cantrell's soft moonlight and magnolias drawl disappeared, only to be replaced with the slightly twangier hill-country accent more like Stenton's and Nancy Ayers's.

It hadn't occurred to Ethan that at least some of the people in the room had more or less grown up together. Harold Dennis was older than the Powers brothers, but by less than a decade. He, Michelle Fraser and Kayla Powers were the outsiders in this group.

And Kayla and Delray Powers were the two with the most at stake, if what Michelle told him about the wills were to hold true.

It was time for him to deal with the two of them, one-on-one.

While the others squabbled, he turned to Michelle Fraser. "Would you and your client please accompany us to the office?" When she nodded, he turned to Delray and asked, "You, too, if you have the time?"

"No one is under arrest here, am I correct?" Michelle asked, her tone cautious but confident.

Ethan shook his head. "No one is under arrest. I would simply like the opportunity to talk to each of the principal beneficiaries of the two wills." He turned back to Delray. "You're welcome to bring an attorney of your choosing along if it would make you feel more comfortable."

"I'll go with you," Harold Dennis said, breaking away from the other conversation.

But Del shook his head. "No, Uncle Hal, would you stay here, please?" He glanced over at the door as if he expected a better candidate to walk through. When no one appeared, he drew a deep breath and gave the older man a confident nod. "I think it would be better if you were to stay here in the office. Rumors will be flying around, and we need somebody steady at the helm now more than ever. If you would stay here with my dad, I don't mind accompanying the lieutenant to the sheriff's offices." He turned to Michelle. "I won't ask you to sit with me, though, because I don't want there to be any possibility someone would say you had a conflict of interest. Who would you recommend I bring?"

"If Chet Barrow is here, I think he would be a good choice," Michelle told him. "He needs something to focus on, and despite his posturing, he is a bright kid. He'll help you navigate anything you feel uncomfortable talking through."

Del nodded. "Good call."

"I'm assuming you'll want to follow us in your own vehicles?" Ethan asked.

"Yes," Michelle said briskly. When Del nodded, Ethan turned to Sheriff Stenton. "Okay if I leave you here to secure the scene?"

The sheriff was already ushering Senator Powers and Natalie Cantrell to the door. "I'll stay on-site until my deputy is here. Join you shortly."

Ethan nodded. "Sounds like a plan."

He approached Nancy Ayers's desk, his most affable smile in place. "Ma'am, could I prevail upon you to get some sort of a tote bag or duffel bag I might use to carry this out without drawing attention to myself?" He raised the bag containing the handgun for her to see.

"Oh!" She fluttered a hand to her chest, then nodded. "Of course. One moment."

Ethan watched her paw through desk drawers. At last, she pulled a canvas tote bag with a grocery store logo from her bottom drawer. "Will this do?"

Then, before he could reach for it, she nearly snatched it back. "Wait, what am I thinking? You need something better than this to carry something like—"

"Actually, no, it's perfect." He extended a hand for the bag. "If I walk out of here with a machine gun case people might start talking."

The older woman gave a nervous laugh, then thrust the bag into his hand. She pressed her palm to her heart again and shook her head. "Right. I'm sorry. I was being ridiculous," she babbled. "I can't believe what's happening—"

"Totally understandable," he said soothingly. "And you weren't ridiculous, you were helpful and I appreciate it," he said sincerely. "Can I count on you to help the sheriff secure the area?"

Nancy straightened as if he'd pinned a deputy's star to her floral blouse. "Absolutely."

"Thank you, ma'am."

With a small, tight smile, he took the tote bag containing the handgun from Tyrone Powers's safe and marched to the stairs, trusting all the interested parties would soon follow.

"YOU'RE SAYING YOU didn't know the contents of either last will and testament before Mr. Dennis called the meeting?" Ethan clarified, leaning in to look Del Powers straight in the eye.

"Asked and answered," the annoying young lawyer with the over-styled hair seated next to Del replied in a dismissive tone.

They sat in the closet of an office he'd been using at the county detention center. Since this was an informal interview, all parties agreed it was okay to leave the door open so the room wouldn't feel too closed in.

Thankfully, Del ignored the man who'd introduced himself as Chet Barrow and answered. "No. Not exactly. I mean, I always knew at some point it would be Trey and me running the place, but I never expected to be the managing partner," he said, giving his head a slow shake. "It's like when you're the prince who's born third or fourth in line to the throne, you know?"

Beside him, Barrow gave a snort, but no further comment.

"You mean a line of succession?" Ethan hazarded.

Del nodded. "I figured it would pass to Trey and eventually he would have a couple of kids and they'd jump in line ahead of me." He gave a short, sharp laugh. "My whole life is planned out for me to work my way down the ladder."

A loud guffaw escaped Barrow, but he made no objection to his client's commentary.

"I've never considered myself a particularly ambitious person." Del shrugged. "There wasn't any competition between Trey and me."

"No?"

The younger man gave them a wan smile. "I knew from the time we were kids it was never supposed to be me. Trey was the anointed one, and I was happy to go along for the ride. Nobody expected much of me and as long as I showed up where and when I was told and didn't do anything to make my dad look bad... Overall, it's been a pretty good life."

Ethan considered his statement for a moment, doubt niggling at him. He was so ambitious; it was hard to imagine someone so admittedly...not. "And even now you don't want to be the one with all the power?"

Del gave a short, humorless laugh. "No."

"You sound pretty sure," Ethan said, instantly skeptical about anyone who would be so cavalier about tossing away wealth and the access money can buy. Then again, he hadn't been born with either. Del Powers had, and he would never want for either. Maybe if you always had influence and were confident you always would, you might not feel the need to fight for more. Being a Powers was a given in Del's life, regardless of who was actually running the law firm.

But something about Del told him the young man was not entirely confident about his position in the family.

"Tell me about your relationship with your cousin Trey."

"My relationship with Trey?" the young man asked, clearly surprised to be asked about anything so personal.

"Yeah," Ethan said, trying to keep the conversation on a more casual footing. "You were about the same age. Were y'all close?"

Del eyed him with a lawyer's skepticism and slid a glance at the man beside him before he answered. "We didn't run with the same crowd, but we weren't *not* close."

Ethan fought the urge to laugh at the backbends the guy was willing to do to avoid saying a simple *no*. "When you say he ran with a different crowd, how would you characterize your cousin's friends?"

"His friends?" He paused for a moment as if weighing the harm in answering. "I don't know many of them well."

"Your impressions, then." He flashed a coaxing smile. "I'm not asking for testimony. I only want to get a feel for who he was running with. Were they serious or partiers?"

Del snorted, and Chet rolled his eyes. "I think you know they were partiers," Del said, his ears turning red.

"And you're not?"

The young man sat up, and Ethan knew he'd delivered the perfect strike to the kid's masculine ego. "I can party if I want to. I choose to do other things with my time."

"Right, of course." Ethan lounged back in the chair. "What sort of hobbies do you enjoy?" he asked, but his attention was drawn to some movement outside his office door.

He spotted Kayla Powers and Michelle Fraser taking seats not far away from where he was speaking to Del.

"I hike a lot," Del said with a shrug. "Fish, hunt. The usual."

"Boating?" Ethan prompted, though his attention remained divided.

"Not as into the boating as Trey was," Del answered briefly. "I prefer nonmotorized watercraft. Canoes, kayaking, that sort of thing."

"Oh, yeah. Me, too," Ethan said, forcing his attention back to the young man seated across from him.

"Sure you do," Chet Barrow muttered. "Can we move this along?"

Unfazed by the other attorney's impatience, Ethan kept his focus on Del. "I grew up not far from the Buffalo River. I consider it my happy place."

Del nodded as if he understood the feeling entirely. "I like going up to the lake house, but I'm happier paddling around in the coves than speeding around on the lake."

Ethan thought about the sleek red ski boat Trey Powers had been driving the night Mallory Murray went overboard and ended up drowning in Table Rock Lake.

"Were you with your cousin the night of the boating accident?" he asked.

"Objection," Barrow spouted, sitting up out of his slouch.

"We aren't in court, counselor," Ethan said evenly. "It was a simple question, and Mr. Powers's response would in no way incriminate him."

Del shook his head. "No, I wasn't with them the night of the accident. As a matter of fact, I was out of town the whole weekend."

Ethan nodded. "Oh, right." He flashed a sheepish smile. "I think I remember reading as much in the report."

"I told the detective in charge of the case when she interviewed me."

"Grace Reed," Ethan said with a sage nod. Chet Barrow grunted at the mention of the name, so he couldn't resist pushing a bit. "She's one of our best."

"Is this relevant to the disposal of Tyrone Powers's estate?" Barrow asked officiously.

Ethan didn't answer. Instead, he let the tense silence stretch until Del shifted in his seat.

"I have to agree with Chet. I don't know what any of this has to do with Uncle Ty's will," Del said briskly.

Shrugging, Ethan allowed him to steer the conversation back at last. "I'm more concerned about your uncle's death… Your uncle and your cousin's deaths…" he amended. "Do you know if maybe your cousin was keeping company with anyone who would have wished him ill?"

"We've already covered this ground, Lieutenant," Barrow interjected.

Del opened his hands in a gesture of futility. "I told Agent Reed and Sheriff Stenton everything I know about the people Trey hung around. Granted, there were a lot fewer these days than there were before his arrest, but he still had a pretty substantial circle of friends."

He put a little emphasis on the last word, and it made Ethan look up sharply.

"But you don't think they were good and real friendships?" he hazarded.

"Calls for speculation on a topic Mr. Powers knows nothing about," Barrow interrupted.

"I'm asking his opinion, and again, we are not in court," Ethan returned calmly. "But feel free not to answer if it makes you uncomfortable, Mr. Powers," he added, cutting a glance at the young man beside him.

Del glanced at Barrow, then sat up straighter. "I don't think Trey was interested in developing good and real friendships, Lieutenant. My cousin was all about appearances. That's why he was so upset the night of the Powers Family Foundation gala."

"How would you know?" Chet asked, his tone dripping with disdain.

Red flags of color lit Del's face, but the young man didn't back down. "You can go, Chet."

Barrow's jaw dropped. He was clearly not accustomed to being dismissed. "What?"

"Go ahead and head back to the office. I'll be back shortly."

The attorney opened and closed his mouth a couple of times, before curling his lip into a sneer. "You know what? Okay, fine."

Ethan scratched his jaw, than crossed his arms over his chest, trying not to be too obvious in his gloating as the young attorney gathered his things, muttering under his breath the whole time.

Del remained silent, too, a look of stubborn stoicism blanking all emotion from his face as the other man fumed. In his studied nonreactivity, Ethan could see exactly how Del Powers had survived in his cousin's shadow.

When Barrow was gone, Ethan propped his elbows on the desk and leaned in. "Trey was upset the night of the gala. People were talking about him."

Del nodded. "People have been talking about him for months, but I don't think he expected them to have the guts to do it at a function sponsored by our family."

Ethan nodded as if digesting the notion. "It would be galling."

"I'm sure you've heard he said some unkind things to Kayla," Del said with little inflection in his tone.

"Yes. She told us they had exchanged some words at the Foundation gala."

"More like Trey had some things to say, and Kayla stood there and took it," Del said succinctly. "Believe me, most of the time it's easier to let it roll right off you."

"You don't seem to bear the same animosity toward Mrs. Powers as other members of your family do," Ethan observed quietly.

"I didn't realize anybody bore any animosity toward Kayla at all until the past couple of days," Del said with a shrug. "Uncle Ty seemed happy. I thought Dad was okay with everything. He didn't raise any objections when the two of them got married."

"Do you think your uncle would have hesitated if your father had objected?"

Del gave a short laugh. "Lieutenant, my father might be a US Senator, but he was still the second son," he said, fixing Ethan with a pointed stare. "Who do you think held the balance of power in the Powers brothers' relationship?"

"I assume you mean your Uncle Tyrone."

"Bingo."

"Were you surprised Trey turned on Mrs. Powers at the gala?"

"Surprised?" Del shook his head. "No. Not surprised. Trey was feeling backed into a corner, and whenever Trey didn't get his way, he had a tendency to lash out. Kayla happened to be standing nearby, but it could have been any one of us in the line of fire."

"You realize you're the only member of your family who isn't pointing the finger at your uncle's second wife," Ethan said bluntly, hoping to throw the young man off-balance with his candor.

"I'm not *not* pointing a finger either," Del answered blandly. "Aunt Natalie was also no saint. She likes to sweep in here and act like she was the woman usurped, but she was the one who left Uncle Ty. She had a better offer on the table."

"From everything I hear, there is no better offer than to be a member of the Powers family."

"In Northwest Arkansas, maybe," Del answered, letting his derision for how the family was perceived show plainly on his face for a brief moment. "But let's be honest here, Lieutenant, this is a small pond. We may be big fish up here, but anywhere else outside our sphere of influence?" He shook his head, then looked away. "It's a big world out there. Most of us don't stray outside of our little corner of it often. We like being the big fish in the small pond, and stepping out, even if it's someplace as middling as Little Rock, only reminds us of how small we are in the big picture."

"I understand." Convinced he'd fished this particular small pond enough for the time being, Ethan extended a hand. "I appreciate you coming down here to talk to me one-on-one."

Delray Powers shook Ethan's hand, then rose, buttoning the jacket of his bespoke suit in a single practiced movement. "Any information on when we might be able to proceed with arrangements?"

Ethan gave him a weary smile. "I'm afraid that information will go directly to Mrs. Powers, but I'm sure she'll be in contact to make certain everything is done to the family's satisfaction."

"I know it's all circumstantial and you don't have anything hard to go on at this point," Del began, then darted a glance at the door. "But you have to admit it's all pretty coincidental, don't you?"

"Sometimes a coincidence is simply a coincidence," Ethan stated. "My job is to determine whether enough of those circumstances add up to something real and tangible. If they do, and we can find proof to back up our suspicions beyond a reasonable doubt, you can bet we will hold the responsible party accountable for their actions."

Del bobbed his head. "Thank you, Lieutenant. I'd better get back to the office and see what I can do to smooth Uncle Hal's ruffled feathers."

"Your feathers are remarkably unruffled," Ethan said as he stepped around the desk to see the other man out.

"Hard to miss what you've never expected to have, Lieutenant," he said, sending a wan look at Michelle and Kayla as the two men left the small office. "PP&W was never supposed to end up in my hands, and frankly, I'm somewhat relieved it never will."

"Never say never," Michelle Fraser said as she rose from her perch on the edge of a cubicle desk. "If someone has their way it could be passing into your hands faster than you ever imagined." She flashed a half smile. "I saw Chet leave. You doing okay, Del?"

"Yes. There was no reason to keep him here."

"He's shaken," Michelle said, and Ethan couldn't help but admire her kindness. He couldn't say he'd be as patient with the obnoxious young attorney. "He would have done anything for Trey."

"I think we're all trying to get our bearings," Del allowed.

Michelle glanced over at Kayla, then back at Del. "Nice summation, counselor. Now, do me a favor and make sure I still have a job to come back to this afternoon?"

"You still have a job," both Del and Kayla responded without hesitation.

The four of them shared a laugh, then exchanged hugs and handshakes once again. As they watched Del walk toward the exit, Ethan asked, "Sheriff Stenton still keeping the peace?"

"I asked him to hang back for a few minutes to give us a chance to talk to you alone," Michelle answered, her eyes fixed on Del's retreating figure.

"Oh?"

Kayla rose from the desk chair, her expression as curious as his must have been. "You can't be seriously worried about your job," she said, her brows knit.

Michelle sighed heavily, then hooked a hand through an arm of each of them, turning them back to the glorified broom closet Ethan was calling an office. "No. But I do need to talk to you about my job," she said as she urged them forward.

Ethan stepped aside, allowing them to precede him into the room. "Oh?"

"Yes. Close the door if you would, please," Michelle asked as she propelled Kayla to a chair.

Ethan followed her instruction, then waited until they were both settled into their chairs before circling the desk and reclaiming his own seat. He watched as the bright, sharp attorney seated across from him drew a deep, surprisingly shaky breath. "You aren't quitting are you?" he cajoled.

"Quitting? No." She grimaced as she looked over at Kayla. "Or, well, maybe. Sort of."

"What do you mean?" Kayla demanded.

Something coiled in his gut, but it was the good sort of anticipation. "Go on," he prompted.

"I think, in light of this morning's revelations, and the possibility of a power struggle taking place within the walls of Powers, Powers & Walton, the time has come for me to talk to you both about my real job."

Chapter Twelve

"Your real job?"

Michelle could feel Kayla's probing gaze as she asked the question, but she was unable to tear her eyes from Ethan Scott. The corner of his mouth twitched and she had the distinct impression he was smothering a smug smile. She couldn't blame him.

He'd been right about her all along.

While she never intended to blow her own cover, the events of the morning made her realize she was going to have to call an audible in order to be able to wrap up her case the way she wanted to. Kayla Powers was in charge, for now, and she had Kayla on her side. If Tyrone's wills got tangled up in probate, it was entirely possible a judge would appoint a mediator or a third party with no familial connection as managing partner of PP&W until the will situation could be unraveled.

Michelle couldn't wait. She needed to get the information she'd come for and get the heck out of there.

With Kayla at the helm, Michelle figured she could simply ask for the access she'd been trying to gain for the better part of a year. And with Ethan Scott and the Arkansas Criminal Investigation Division backing her up, she might be able to exonerate her client while shutting down what could possibly be one of the larger illegal campaign finance schemes currently operating in the States.

To do all that, she had to admit Ethan Scott and Grace Reed had been right about her all along. She was a cop down to the soles of her feet.

Recruited by the Federal Bureau of Investigation while still in law school, she worked for the Bureau for the better part of those two years she claimed to have been touring Europe. As a forensic accounting expert, she'd become the Bureau's lead investigator working with the Federal Election Commission.

Senator William Powers's seemingly unlimited war chest of campaign funding was a hot topic in DC oversight circles. Not many people expected to find wealth in a state like Arkansas—particularly not in the rural Ozark Mountain region.

Sure, everybody knew the state was home to the world's largest retailer, but they were unaware the area was also home to massive shipping and logistics companies as well as food processing conglomerates. When she first started looking into the possibility of campaign finance violations in Senator Powers's organization, she'd been surprised as well.

It had taken some convincing to get her elitist East Coast superiors to realize there was money flowing through them there hills.

"I am Special Agent Michelle Fraser, on loan from the FBI and working for the Federal Election Commission's investigatory branch," she said in a low, confidential tone. "I have been working undercover at PP&W in an attempt to discover how the firm was circumventing election contribution laws and feeding Senator Powers's campaigns with unreported contributions."

Kayla sucked in a sharp breath, and Michelle turned to look at her client. "I assure you I am a qualified attorney who is fully prepared to mount any defense you might need against any charges brought against you in the death of Tyrone Powers Junior and Tyrone Powers the third," she stated unequivocally.

"You were investigating him?" Kayla asked, sounding wounded by the idea.

Michelle shook her head. "No, ma'am. I don't believe your husband was directly involved in any kind of impropriety. I can't say if Trey might have been. My investigation hasn't allowed me access to the encrypted files we need to see exactly who was moving money between accounts."

Ethan Scott leaned forward, propping his forearms on the edge of the desk and threading his fingers together. "What can we do for you?"

Michelle didn't look away from Kayla. "I need your help. I'm afraid the window of opportunity may be closing on both of us."

"What do you mean?" Kayla asked.

"It's clear somebody is trying to frame you for these murders," she stated bluntly. "I don't know if the killings themselves were committed by a professional or by someone you know, but I will bet dollars to doughnuts the gun that dropped out Tyrone's safe this afternoon is the same weapon used to kill both men."

She chanced a glance in Ethan's direction and found him nodding. "I agree," he said. "I've asked them to expedite the ballistics on it. But the gun won't give us anything more concrete than we already have."

Michelle and Kayla both nodded. As defense attorneys they were well aware getting usable, conclusive evidence from a gun was unlikely. They'd be able to determine if the gun had been fired recently, but not exactly when. They could match bullets to those used to kill Tyrone and Trey, but not whether they came from a particular gun. And everything people saw on television about the ability to lift clear fingerprints from a gun was largely fiction.

"It could give you more circumstantial evidence," Kayla said softly.

"And it is starting to pile up." Michelle reached over and gave the other woman's wrist a reassuring squeeze. "I believe whoever is involved in the campaign finance scheme may be connected to the murders."

"Always follow the money," Ethan Scott said gravely.

"Exactly."

"But how? You've been at PP&W for years," Kayla said, her bewilderment evident in every word. "Wouldn't you have figured it out by now?"

"I never said it was easy. The biggest hurdle has been my inability to work freely within the firm's mainframe system," Michelle assured her. "PP&W has a far more sophisticated data security system than most law firms. Running into their maze of technology was one of the things that tipped me off about the firm's involvement."

"You're some kind of computer genius, too?" Kayla asked, incredulous.

"I did my undergraduate work in information technology. I'd originally planned to go into copyright and patent law with an eye on working in the tech industry."

"But then the Feds came calling," Ethan interjected. "Who wouldn't choose a graded government salary over the pittance those struggling social media moguls are paying?"

Michelle shot him a quelling glance, but kept her focus on Kayla. She could exchange snarky commentary with him later. Right now, she had to convince the new managing partner of PP&W to give her carte blanche.

"I'm close. I'm so close, but I'm restricted as to the time I can spend on the firm server without drawing suspicion."

"I'm still trying to wrap my head around the whole thing," Kayla said wonderingly. "I saw your résumé. I told Tyrone you looked like a good candidate. I convinced him female defense attorneys go over better with juries. So much for trusting my feminist instincts."

"Your instincts were right," Michelle said without a trace of rancor. "I am a damn good defense attorney, as my track record has proven. But yes, the résumé you saw was…incomplete."

"Obviously," she said dryly.

"Kayla, I've been working my way up in this firm, gaining the trust of people like Harold Dennis and your husband so I could get this far. We have an opportunity here," she said, maintaining direct eye contact with her client. "With your say-so, I can access any file I may need and get out. If I've narrowed it down correctly, I should be able to have all of the data I need to determine exactly who is involved and to what extent."

"What do you want from me?" Kayla asked.

"I need you to clear the decks for a day, maybe two."

"And by clear the decks you mean…?" Kayla's brows rose.

"I mean close the firm for a couple days. Tell everyone you're taking the rest of the week off out of respect for Ty and Trey, and to allow the family to prepare for the services."

She turned and looked at Ethan Scott. "Any time line on when the bodies might be released?"

"Probably within the next 24 to 48 hours," he responded. "I can put in a call."

"Tyrone wanted to be cremated," Kayla said blankly. "They're not going to allow me to do so this quickly."

Ethan Scott nodded. "We would ask you to transport the bodies to a local funeral home to be held until the coroner's report is complete, but if you wish to conduct a memorial service there's no reason to delay. I would advise against an open casket."

Kayla shuddered. "No," she whispered. "I don't care what Natalie says about Trey's service, but I don't want anyone to see Tyrone the way I saw him."

"Do you agree it would be a good idea to close the firm for a few days?" Michelle pressed.

Kayla's gaze snapped to hers. "Is this actually happening? Am I about to take the helm of a sinking ship?" she asked.

"Not necessarily," Michelle was quick to interject.

"Tyrone took such great pride in the family firm. His father built it. He couldn't wait to hand over the reins to Trey one day," she said, her voice breaking. "I'm glad he's not here to hear all this. I'm glad he won't have his heart broken this way."

Michelle turned back to Ethan. "Do you see where I'm going with this?"

He nodded. "What do you need from me?"

She shook her head. "I need you to continue with the murder investigation as you would normally. I need

Kayla to remain the primary suspect as far as the world is concerned, but I also need you to start looking in other directions as well."

"The possibility of a professional hit had crossed my mind," he admitted. "And one ordered as a cover-up of some kind would lend credence to the theory."

A soft whimper escaped Kayla, but Michelle didn't have time to soften their conversation to protect delicate feelings. "A distinct possibility. This is why I need to dig into the money. I need to see if all of it's going to the senator's campaigns, or if it's being shunted through there as a front for something else."

"We're going back in there," Kayla said. "To the office?"

"We have to. You have to establish you are in control of the firm."

"I don't feel like I'm in control of anything at the moment." She barked a short laugh of disbelief. "Until five minutes ago, I thought you worked for PP&W."

"Technically, I do. And I know I don't have to tell Lieutenant Scott this, but in case you don't understand exactly what happened here, I went off script. If my superior finds out I revealed myself and my mission to the two of you, after two years of deep cover, I would most certainly be out of a job."

Kayla nodded, but her dazed expression left plenty of room for concern.

Michelle shot Ethan a look, wondering if she'd done the right thing by taking them into her confidence. He gave her a brief nod of reassurance.

"What's your plan?" he asked brusquely.

"I'll need access to the offices while everyone else is gone. I'll probably need some sort of cover story for the actual IT department. I'll dummy up a notice of a scheduled maintenance outage on one of the main software systems. One that's network-based, rather than an internet portal."

Ethan pursed his lips. "Sounds reasonable, but don't those usually happen in the overnight hours?" he asked, concern furrowing his brow.

Michelle shrugged. "Wouldn't be the first all-nighter I've pulled and probably won't be the last."

"It won't be safe for you to be in there alone late at night," he stated flatly.

"It's a law firm after hours, not a highway underpass. I'm probably safer there at 2 a.m. than I am at 2 p.m.," she said, casting a sidelong glance at Kayla.

"True," the other woman murmured, though she was clearly lost in thought.

"I'll come down there with you," he insisted.

She shook her head. "You'd be a hindrance. If I'm caught down there alone, I can say I couldn't sleep and was working on a case file. How would I explain your presence?"

"I need to get out of the hotel," Kayla said, giving voice to what had been preoccupying her, oblivious to their conversation.

"We can arrange a cleaning company for the house," Michelle offered, grateful to pivot away from Lieutenant Scott's daydreams of crashing her undercover party at PP&W.

Kayla wagged her head back and forth. "I can't go back there. We'll have to have it done, but I'm not going back there. Ever."

"Perhaps you'd be more comfortable renting a house,"

Ethan suggested. "Maybe one of those owner vacation rental situations?"

"Maybe," Kayla said, her voice soft and raspy.

"Or you could rent a place on Beaver Lake," Michelle suggested. "Maybe find a little peace and quiet in the middle of all this."

"The lake," Kayla repeated, her head jerking upward as if yanked by a string. "I could go to the lake house."

Michelle started when she realized what her client was truly saying. "You mean you want to go to the Powers family lake house?"

Kayla nodded. "Yes. After all, Ty did leave his interest in it to me. It's partially mine now, by law. Or it will be when we're though probate. If I'm going to bluster my way into running the firm in the interim, I might as well go for the house, too."

"Wouldn't you rather be closer to town? Arrangements will need to be made, and—"

"I can work with Nancy on the service. Trust me, once I say 'go,' there won't be much for me to do other than show up at the time she tells me."

Michelle had no doubt of that. But she had big doubts about Kayla staying at an isolated house nearly an hour away.

"Do you think it's such a great idea to be in a property you hold jointly with Senator Powers?" Ethan asked, voicing her concerns.

"Particularly after his reactions this morning," Michelle chimed in.

Kayla's eyes sharpened as she looked first to her, then Ethan. "If you think about it there should be no safer place. I can make it known to everyone in the family I intend to use the house for the foreseeable future.

Bill will avoid me for fear of being seen in the company of the suspicious widow. But I don't want any of them to be able to say they were unaware I was in residence. Given this morning's confrontation, if something…untoward were to happen to me, they would automatically be on the suspect list. As for my place on the list, the police are well acquainted with the security system and what it's capable of capturing. I can give them full access to monitor my whereabouts via the security company."

Ethan and Michelle exchanged a glance. Still, Michelle felt uneasy about her client staying alone in such an isolated spot. "Would you agree to having a sheriff's deputy on-site with you?"

Kayla let one shoulder rise and fall and then gave a negligent shrug. "Sure. They can have access to the guesthouse."

Ethan pulled out his phone. "Let me talk to Sheriff Stenton. Not only do we need to keep up the appearance you are still our primary suspect—"

"Which technically, I am," Kayla interrupted.

He tilted his head as if conceding the point. "Technically, you are. Either way, I agree, I'd feel better about you being out there if there was an officer nearby."

"Truthfully, that makes three of us," Kayla admitted. "Admitting as much makes me sad. I've never been afraid to be alone at the lake house. It was always a haven for me."

"We don't have any reason to believe you'd be in danger out there," Ethan was quick to reassure her.

Michelle was forced to agree. "I'd say you're in no greater danger there than you would be here. At least there, you'd have some protection from the press.

Maybe you should consider hiring a temporary guard for the gate."

Kayla shook her head. "I'll go out there with whoever the sheriff can spare. If the press finds me, then I'll address the security issue. For the time being I'd like to keep this as low-key as possible."

Michelle nodded. "I understand."

She shifted in her seat uncomfortably, feeling oddly torn between her two worlds. Part of her didn't want to care about Kayla Powers or the people she left behind at PP&W, but now she was almost out, she had to admit they did matter to her. And those feelings were damn inconvenient. She'd forgotten how hard it was to be two people at once. Other than the brief moments when she had contact with her relay agent, there were times when she could almost forget she wasn't simply an attorney who specialized in criminal defense, working for PP&W.

But she was more, and those worlds were about to collide.

"I'll make sure we get you settled at the lake house, and you have everything you need." They shared a pointed look. Out of the corner of her eye she saw Ethan sit up and take notice, but she rushed on in hopes of covering. "Groceries, anything like that. If you want me to pick up any additional clothing from the house—"

Kayla shook her head. "I have clothes at the lake house. I should be good for a while."

"Then we need to head back to the offices and make it clear you plan to be the one in charge. I have a feeling the longer we leave Harold Dennis to his machinations, the more entrenched he'll become."

Kayla drew a deep breath, then nodded. "Not sure how much deeper he can bury himself in PP&W business, but yes, we need to make it clear he can't simply wave me away."

"And you'll make the announcement about the firm to be closing for the rest of the week?"

Kayla nodded and pushed from her chair. "Yes, I'll tell those with active cases to plan on working remotely if they can't get a continuance."

"Then I'll make sure the email concerning a network outage goes straight to the IT manager. When Benny brings it to your attention, sign off on him distributing the information to the rest of the firm."

As they rose, Ethan Scott did as well. "When do you plan on going into the offices to access the files?" he asked, directing the question specifically to her.

"I can't be sure. Aside from scheduling the outage, I need to lay some groundwork first."

"Will you let me know when you're going in?" he asked.

"Probably not," she answered, meeting his gaze squarely. "I can handle myself, Lieutenant Scott."

"I have no doubt you can, Ms. Fraser," he said, emphasizing the use of the title rather than her actual rank. "But all of us need backup at some time."

"If I do, I'll let you know."

"Best answer I can hope for, I guess," he said dryly. Gesturing to the door, he added, "I would appreciate it if both of you ladies would keep me in the loop as far as any information you come across relating to my investigation."

"Of course we will," Michelle assured him.

Kayla hesitated at the door. "I don't want to be one to cast aspersions on other people, but might I suggest you both take a closer look at the client that owns the private plane Bill and Harold used the night of the gala?"

"The client?" Ethan asked, clearly on high alert.

"Yes. It is a relatively new client called DevCo. Harold brought them on board. They are a real estate development company. I'm not sure exactly what was going on with them, but something about their business made Ty uncomfortable."

"He said as much to you?" Lieutenant Scott persisted.

Kayla nodded. "Not explicitly, but he made comments about them. I know he felt some of their practices might not be entirely aboveboard."

"You say Harold Dennis was the one who brought this client into the firm?" Ethan asked as he walked back to his desk to make a note.

"Correct. They're based out of Oklahoma, I believe, but they have a lot of property in Northwest Arkansas. If I recall correctly, the man who owns it made his money in oil, but his son has a passion for the land business."

"Names?" Ethan asked.

But Kayla only shook her head. "I can't recall them at the moment." She gestured to her head. "It's kind of a mess up there right now, but if they come to me, I'll let you know." Eyes widening, she glanced at Michelle. "Or they'd be in the client files. It shouldn't be too difficult for you to get their information."

"I'll look into it," Michelle promised.

Ethan set his pen down. "I'd appreciate that."

Michelle frowned as she turned back to Kayla. "Do

you believe this was one of the things making Tyrone uneasy about Harold Dennis?"

"I think Harold saw himself as a rainmaker for the firm. This was a big-money client. He told Ty they might be his ticket to retirement. Or so Ty told me," she added with a wry smile. "But if you know anything about the Powers family, you know they consider themselves to be the big shot real estate tycoons around these parts." Her lips twisted into a smirk. "It could have been nothing more than Ty feeling his throne was being threatened."

Michelle thought back to the research she had done on the Powers family and how they came to amass the generational wealth they now enjoyed.

The first Tyrone Powers had started from humble beginnings—worked as a logger, then a builder, and put himself through law school before making his way in the world by representing the interests of landowners and other entrepreneurs such as himself. He'd made friends with all the area movers and shakers and considered himself to be one of them. It was a sense of entitlement he'd passed on to both of his sons.

"Thank you. I'll follow that money trail, too," she assured Ethan, then raised a hand in farewell. "I'll keep in touch."

"Please do," he replied, his voice soft but his gaze penetrating.

Michelle escorted her client through the municipal building and back out into the parking area surrounded by razor wire. Once they reached Michelle's car, they strapped in, waiting for the vents to deliver some much-needed cool air. When she glanced over and found her client eyeballing her, Michelle leaned back. "What?"

"There's some kind of connection between you and the lieutenant," Kayla said, unable to keep the amusement from her voice. "At first, I thought it was nothing more than basic pheromones. I mean, the man is not hard on the eyes," she said slyly. "But now I see it's…"

When Kayla didn't go on, Michelle couldn't resist asking. "See what?"

"There's something more there than simple attraction. More like an understanding."

Michelle thought back to Ethan's insistence they were of a like mind. She was still ruminating when Kayla interrupted with her conclusion.

"You are similar, I guess. You both take the same direct approach with people. There's little fancy footwork with either of you."

Her assessment startled a laugh from Michelle. "Gee, thanks."

"I actually meant it as a compliment," Kayla said with her soft laugh. "You know how it is with most attorneys. We'd rather dance a jig around a topic than give a direct answer."

"But not you," Michelle pointed out. "You couldn't give the police evidence fast enough."

"Because I know my conscience was clear and my life is on the line," Kayla shot back. "Obfuscating would only make me look even more guilty than they were inclined to believe I was already."

"True."

Michelle backed out of the parking space without making further comment on her client's observations. She had enough to worry about in the next forty-eight hours. Everything she'd been working on for the past two years was coming to a head. She couldn't dwell on thoughts of Lieutenant Scott, or whether they might actually be as alike as he believed them to be. She had to find the key evidence she needed to make her case, so she could get back to her real life.

Whatever it would look like after this was done.

Chapter Thirteen

Michelle punched the code Kayla had pulled from Tyrone's files into the alarm system. The vestibule of the PP&W office was lit by nighttime security lights. Beyond them, the hulking shadows of furniture loomed in the yellowish pools of light cast by low wattage bulbs. She kept close to the walls so as not to cast shadows of her own. Not for the first time, she was grateful she'd been assigned an office away from the wall of windows facing out onto the county courthouse. The other attorneys fought for them, but the interior space suited her needs. And on this particular occasion, it saved her from having to commando crawl through the deserted office space.

Like a cat burglar out of a television show, she was dressed in black from head to toe. She even had a black ball cap pulled down over her hair. As she unlocked her office door she wondered if she would keep the funky hair color she'd selected for this particular persona or go back to her own natural shade of dirty blond.

Inside her office, she hit the thumb lock on the knob and hurried to her desk. Rather than taking a seat in the chair she pushed it aside and dropped down to the floor where she extracted her laptop from her bag. She spent the next few seconds booting up, making sure she had power connected and plugging an old-fashioned Ethernet cable into the dongle she attached to her computer. She wanted a hardwired internet connection to ensure a smooth data transfer.

True to her word, Kayla had gone back to the PP&W offices and walked in as if she had been born the boss.

Senator Powers and Natalie Cantrell had already departed, according to Nancy Ayers. The nervous assistant had not seen Del return to the office even though he'd left the sheriff's offices well before they did. No doubt he was touching base with his father off-site.

Only Harold Dennis had remained in the building, his door closed. She nodded to the deputy sitting in a chair outside Tyrone Powers's former office. Nancy informed them a team had come in to process the office for evidence. A single strip of yellow police tape was now stretched across the doorframe. She'd left Kayla in Nancy's capable hands and run down the stairs to her office to start setting up the bogus network outage.

Now, as she keyed her way into the server, Michelle marveled at the skill with which Kayla had handled Harold Dennis. At first, the older man had been contentious. He'd been unwilling to leave his office, claiming he had known Tyrone his entire life, and he'd be damned if he'd leave his protégé's legacy to a woman who married her boss.

Kayla remained calm. She'd explained to Harold that she felt no animosity toward him, nor did she understand where his hostility toward her was coming from. She flattered him, telling the older man she needed his experience and expertise, though Michelle was certain

Kayla was more capable than anyone wanted to give her credit for.

Like the entitled man he was, Harold had eaten it up. When Kayla floated the idea of closing the offices for the remainder of the week so they might pay homage to the family and use the time to make the appropriate arrangements for the memorial services, he readily agreed.

Michelle hummed softly to herself in the darkness, shaking her head at the remembrance of the older man's clear duplicity. The offices might be closed to the public and clients, but it was clear Harold Dennis would not be abandoning his post anytime soon. Which is why it was necessary for Michelle to do her work in the dead of night.

Poor, beleaguered Benny Jenkins, the firm's IT guru, usually spent his days beset by attorneys who somehow managed to blow up their laptops. He liked to grumble about how the attorneys could be smart enough to handle extensive schooling yet couldn't remember to update their security software or log out of the VPN when not actively using network resources. In other words, he was more than amenable to the suggestion of any kind of break.

She'd dummied together an email using the logo of one of their main database providers, then sent it from a cloned email address. He'd replied to the account she set up and confirmed the supposed outage was scheduled to take place that night.

To anyone else it would appear the systems were down, but Michelle had an entire team of IT professionals locked in and ready to start going at the security on the server as soon as the appointed hour rolled around.

The minute her contact gave her the heads-up they were in, she'd start doing her own digging.

Satisfied she'd set herself up for success, she braced her back against the wall and closed her eyes. All she could do now was wait.

Only six minutes had elapsed since the scheduled outage had begun when her phone buzzed. She snatched it up and pressed it to her ear. "Hello?"

"We're in."

"So quickly?"

A chuckle reverberated in her ear. "We're good at what we do."

Michelle exhaled and then grinned. "And thank goodness. Thank your team," she said as she watched her screen fill with data. "I'm in, too. Have we started the upload to the secure server?"

"The upload is almost complete. I had them run it first."

"Ten-four," Michelle replied.

"Let me know when you're out and we'll restore service."

"Will do," Michelle answered, already distracted by the columns and letters and numbers filling her screen.

She ended the call and watched as the transfer of files to the portable hard drive she brought began. The countdown on the computer itself claimed it would take fifteen minutes. She hated hanging around any longer than absolutely necessary, but Michelle wanted the assurance of having the PP&W records in her pocket. She figured this would be her only shot at the files; therefore she could indulge herself in the belt-and-suspenders approach to securing this data. No one would be coming into the office at 1 a.m. Particularly not when Natalie

Cantrell had set her son's memorial service for bright and early the following morning.

Michelle couldn't help wondering if it was because Mrs. Cantrell was anxious to get back to her life in Little Rock as quickly as possible. She didn't seem to be concerned about the inconsequential amount of money Tyrone had stipulated for her in the codicils nobody had bothered to read in Harold Dennis's office. Michelle had been surprised to discover Tyrone had left a part of his estate to the woman who had left him, but Kayla seemed to be utterly unfazed by it.

"A total Ty move," Kayla said with a shrug. "He felt a responsibility for everyone and everything around him. I used to tease him about suffering from oldest child syndrome."

Michelle watched the green progress bar move millimeter by millimeter across the screen. What would records show? Would she find a piece of the puzzle she'd been missing? Would Tyrone Powers prove himself to be as innocent as his wife believed him to be? Was fear of discovery the reason Tyrone and Trey were killed? Would they be able to single out a payment to a possible killer?

She couldn't help thinking about Harold Dennis and the private jet. She'd found DevCo's corporate information easily enough and passed it along to Ethan Scott, but she hadn't heard anything more. But since Kayla had planted the seed about Harold Dennis, she couldn't stop wondering about him.

For decades he'd been the power behind the throne—first, as a young man working for the senior Tyrone, then as the mentor who helped Tyrone III grow into the role. Did he resent being the power behind the Powers family? Or was he simply what he appeared to be—a man destined to do other people's bidding?

A heavy clunking sound broke the still quiet of the sleeping building. Michelle sat up, drawing her legs in, prepared to spring to her feet, but the noise did not come again. She glanced up at the ceiling, then let her gaze travel over the wall to the door. The building was far from new. It was entirely possible what she'd heard was merely a function of the ancient heating and cooling system.

She didn't call out. If there was someone else on the premises, she didn't want them to know she was there. Instead, she lowered the lid of her laptop to a forty-five degree angle to minimize the glow of the screen, and pushed it deeper into the chair well.

Then, she reached a hand into her bag, drew out her service weapon and waited.

All too aware of the slash of dim light the frosted glass running the length of the office door allowed, she angled herself against the desk facing the wall she'd leaned on moments before.

But no other sound came from the space beyond her locked door.

Her heart rate had returned to normal when she heard a different noise. This one was not the metallic *thunk* of machinery. It was more of a scuffling, scratching sound. On alert again, she gripped her weapon tighter, her eyes fixed on a strip of light on the wall. If anyone came near her door, she'd see a shadow in the diffuse light.

She stared hard at it, barely willing to blink in case she missed a hint of movement.

Behind her, the laptop whirred softly. Shifting her weight, she ducked her head and raised the lid. The download had passed the 50 percent mark. Checking her watch, she saw ten minutes had passed since the transfer started. She eyed her phone, tempted to call in to double-check on the upload to the cloud. This was simply a backup to the backup, she reminded herself. Was it worth the heart palpitations?

But she couldn't bring herself to pull the plug on it when it was so close to being complete. She was simply a little spooked.

Pressing back against the desk, she wondered if she should have asked Ethan Scott to come with her. Not because she needed some big, strong man to help her complete her mission, but more to act as her backup. A human thumb drive, of sorts. After all, a person could never have too much backup, right? And if backup also came with broad shoulders, a handsome face, some dry wit and a nine-millimeter, all the better, right?

She chuckled at her own reasoning. Then she amused herself by imagining tucking the handsome cop into her bag alongside her laptop, phone and firearm, and oh so casually strolling out of the PP&W offices once and for all. But though she had envisioned her exit over and over throughout her assignment, it failed to tickle her as much as she thought it would. She would miss Kayla, with her disarming mix of vulnerability and cut-to-the-chase sensibilities.

And Ethan Scott?

She'd likely never lay eyes on the man again. He was based in Arkansas. Born and bred in the Ozarks, and proud of it. She was a former military kid who'd never called any place home for more than a few years.

Her time in the DC area was the closest she'd come to putting down roots, but while her network spread wide, those roots didn't go deep. She kept in touch with a handful of her former classmates from law school, even fewer from her undergrad. She had a colleague or two she knew well enough to grab a drink with when she'd worked in the office, but no doubt their lives had moved on while hers had gone undercover.

When the idea was first pitched to her it sounded so intriguing. There was nothing she loved more than putting together a puzzle. This assignment seemed to have her name written all over it. Not only was she able to use her investigative and legal skills—she could also tap into her knowledge of technology.

Leaning over, she checked the progress bar and smiled when she saw the download was nearly finished. Another glance at her watch reassured her she would indeed have her backup for backup, and then she'd get out of there.

Out of there.

Ethan had asked her to text him when she left the office. She'd warned him it would be in the middle of the night, but he claimed he didn't care. There was no reason to interrupt his night. Not when she'd be heading straight back to her place to dive into data.

She tilted the screen back and watched as the last few kilobytes of data were transferred from the network to the flashing drive. The message she'd been waiting for popped up. Her download was complete. She ejected the drive and retracted it, then sent the agreed-upon text to her contact to let her know she was out.

Insomnia sucks. Taking a pill.

But as she went to drop the memory stick into her bag, something stopped her. The urge to check the data one more time gripped her so hard, she felt almost paralyzed. Figuring the sensation was more likely caused by the numb legs and aching back from sitting on the floor, she crawled out from under the desk. But she couldn't resist the urge to check one more time before she left.

Placing her laptop on the desk, she tilted the lid back until the screen lit her face. She plugged in the drive once more, checking the directory of files to be certain she hadn't transferred anything to the laptop itself, then double-clicked on the directory for the external source. A smile curved her lips as she watched thousands of data files populate the menu screen. She was scrolling to the bottom to see where the final count landed, when she heard the scuffling noise again.

She swore softly under her breath, ejected the drive and dropped it down the front of her shirt before closing the lid on her laptop. She saw no movement against the strip of diffused light bouncing off the office wall, but the tight coiling in her gut told her something was happening. Plunging a hand down the front of her T-shirt, she secured the thumb drive in the band of her bra.

She looped the handles of her bag over her left wrist and rose with her service weapon gripped in her right hand. She'd almost convinced herself she was being foolish, made skittish by bumps in the night in an old building, but the urge to flee was growing stronger by the second.

Then she heard the rattle of someone testing her door handle.

She dropped back to the floor and disengaged the safety on her weapon.

The hairs on the back of her neck rose as she shifted into the chair well. Seconds passed, but they seemed like minutes. She was debating whether she'd actually heard what she thought she heard when a muffled sound crack echoed through the building.

Before she could draw breath, the glass beside her door shattered into pieces. Michelle held her position, her gun at the ready.

Someone swore softly, then she heard the soft snick of a lock being turned. The office door swung open, allowing more of the dim light from the outer office to spill in. The sound of labored breathing drew closer and she held her own. Glass crunched beneath heavy footfalls. Unable to ascertain whether her intruder worked alone or had company, she decided the best course of action was to hold her position.

Sipping oxygen through her nose and barely parted lips, she waited, her hand tight around the grip of her weapon. She tensed every muscle in her body, ready to spring into action. But her intruder stopped on the other side of the desk. Then, they grabbed something—presumably her laptop—from the desk, knocking a stack of client files to the floor as they turned to leave.

Footsteps crunched on the glass again, this time moving faster. Thankfully, whoever it was seemed to be fleeing the scene. The temptation to go after the thief was so strong she had to grit her teeth to ward it off. Her computer was clean as a whistle, she'd made sure it was. Michelle bit her lip as she eased herself out of her hiding spot. The person who'd shot out the glass panel was running now, crashing through the maze of cubicles between her office and the front vestibule.

She reached the opening in time to see a tall figure also clad in dark clothing dash through the dimly lit foyer and out the front door.

Rocking back on her heels, she leaned against the door for support, panting as she stared up at the ceiling and pieced together what had happened.

A man. A man had shot his way into an office that was supposed to be empty. A tall, broad-shouldered man, she realized, forcing her brain to home in on pertinent details. Tall. Dark clothes. Broad shoulders. Not fast, she noted absently. Squeezing her eyes shut she tried to zoom in on the details. He moved quickly, but not easily. Not agile, but not clumsy either. Ungainly.

And who knew she'd be here at this particular hour? Did they think she'd leave her laptop behind with the offices closed for the day? She turned her head to look back at where she'd placed the computer. No laptop. Pressing her hand to her heart, Michelle treated herself to a great big gulp of air as she felt the hard ridge of the removable drive tucked into the elastic band between her breasts.

Okay, so someone had taken her laptop, but they'd be sadly disappointed at what they found there. She exhaled slowly and was trying to muster the energy to get up and get out when another thought struck her. Not a professional.

A pro would have made sure the office was empty. A pro would have come in and taken her out before taking her laptop.

Had her assailant been the same person who shot Tyrone and Trey? Or was he simply someone who figured out she'd been snooping around and wanted to see what she'd found. Could the two incidents be nothing more than coincidence? Not likely.

She needed to know how someone knew she would

be here in the first place. Grabbing her phone, she pulled up Kayla's contact information. But her pulse roared in her ears as her thumb hovered over the call icons.

Kayla.

Kayla and Ethan were the only people who knew she'd be poking around in the PP&W computer system. But the man she'd seen dashing from the building wasn't Ethan Scott. She knew as much down in her bones.

It had to have been someone sent by Kayla—the woman with an alibi for everything.

Her stomach flipped inside out as everything she'd learned about Tyrone Powers's widow in the past two days filtered through her mind. But this time, she forced herself to strip away the presumption of innocence.

Kayla Powers was conveniently away when her husband and his son were brutally murdered in her home. There were no eyewitnesses to attest to her whereabouts. And what about the public confrontation with one of the victims before she left for the lake house? Alone. Only grainy surveillance footage obtained by a security company paid to monitor the premises could exonerate her. She claimed to have been drunk. She'd volunteered evidence and gave the appearance of full cooperation, even though they all knew the forensics testing she'd submitted to was of little prosecutorial value.

Drawing her hand back from the screen, she gnawed her bottom lip as she mulled the possibility. Acting on instinct, she pulled up Ethan Scott's contact information and placed the call.

"Are you out?" he asked by way of greeting.

"No, not exactly," she said, eying the mess around her warily.

"What do you mean, 'not exactly'?"

"I, uh, well, I was on my way out when someone took a shot at me."

"What do you mean 'took a shot at you'?"

"Well, not really at me. At my door. Or rather at the window beside my office door." She frowned as she looked at the wide-open door. "It doesn't make any sense," she said, thinking out loud. "Were they shooting at me?" She turned back to look at her desk. "Maybe they weren't shooting at me."

"I don't think I like the sound of any of this conjecture," Ethan replied shortly. "You need to get the hell out of there."

"He took my laptop."

The non sequitur must have caught him off guard because whatever was coming next in his lecture died away. "Excuse me?"

"My laptop, of all things," she explained. "I dropped to the floor, but it was on the desk. Whoever shot the glass came in, grabbed the laptop and ran."

"They took the computer and ran?"

Michelle nodded. "Couldn't have been a professional. A pro would never have left without making sure I couldn't identify them," she said, still thinking aloud.

"Identify them? Can you identify them?" he persisted.

"Not specifics," she admitted. "Tall, male, a little awkward in their movement, but I can't explain exactly how. It was shadowy, and I could only catch glimpses of him as he ran past security lights."

"Michelle, you need to get out of there now," he said in a low, urgent tone.

"The only people who knew I was going to be here were you and Kayla," she said, her mind whirring like a top.

"Get out of there," he ordered.

"Right." She nodded as the words finally broke through the haze. "Going now."

"Are you sure Kayla and I were the only ones who knew you were heading in there tonight?"

"As far as I know, yes," she informed him. Slipping out of her office, she headed for the door in the same manner in which she entered: sticking close to the walls, avoiding the lights and keeping her head down.

"No contacts at your agency?" he persisted.

"Well, yeah, they knew," she admitted gruffly. "I had an IT team working through my primary contact."

"Any chance your inside person might be the leak?"

"How do I know you aren't?" she shot back.

"You don't, but I'm not."

"Which leaves Kayla," she said.

"Possibly, but Kayla doesn't strike me as anybody's fool. If she were to tip somebody off about your presence in the office tonight or what you might be doing there, it would only reinforce the appearance of her guilt."

"I thought the same thing."

"We've got such a preponderance of circumstantial evidence pointing in her direction right now I sincerely doubt she would be the one to pile on anymore."

"So, you're saying it's not you and it's not Kayla—therefore it must be my contact at the agency."

"I'm saying it's a possibility," Ethan replied. "Are you out yet?"

"Not quite," she answered.

"I'm getting in my car. Isn't there an all-night diner two blocks up from the courthouse?"

"Yes."

"Go there, but stay in your car until I get there. Don't go inside. I'll come to your car," he instructed. "If you get the feeling anyone is following you, keep driving in random patterns, circle blocks, whatever you need to do to get them off your case."

"Ethan?" Michelle didn't like the tremor she heard in her own voice, but at the moment she couldn't even pretend to feel steady.

"Yes?"

"I know how to lose a tail."

"I have no doubt," he assured her. "I'm only saying these things to make myself feel better."

"I figured." She hesitated for a moment, then plunged ahead. "Ethan?"

"I'm here."

"I've never been shot at before," she confessed.

"No?"

"Nope. Have you?"

"A few times," he answered, his voice husky.

"I don't like it," she stated without hesitation.

His chuckle warmed her from the inside out. "I didn't care for it much myself."

She heard the sound of a car ignition. "Are you on your way?"

"I am. Are you out of the building?"

"I am," she replied.

"I'll be at the diner in less than ten minutes. Hang tight."

Keeping her head down she hurried to her vehicle parked two blocks south of the law offices. She waited until her hand touched the handle to unlock her car. The second she was inside she tripped the lock again.

"I'm in my car," she reported.

She heard a whoosh of breath as he exhaled loudly on the other end. "Good deal. Now talk me through what happened again."

Sinking back into the driver seat, Michelle pulled the car out of the spot and headed toward the diner. "I wanted to finish downloading the files to an external drive," she began.

"An external drive? I thought you were uploading to a cloud," he asked.

"I did. I wanted a backup for the backup."

On the other end, Ethan chuckled. "Why am I not surprised?" he asked wryly. "Okay, you got your backup for the backup. What happened next?"

Michelle gripped the wheel tighter as she accelerated through the next intersection. "I heard something. Sounded like someone was trying to open my office door, so I ducked under the desk. The next thing I knew, the glass was shattering. I had my service weapon in my hand, but I was hidden from view. I figured it was best to stay put."

"Unless you were planning to shoot your way out of there, I'd say so."

Michelle let off the gas as the lights of the diner came into view. "I had no plan, but you can bet I would have, if I needed to."

"I have no doubt."

He said the words with a sort of grudging admiration. They warmed her as she pulled into one of the empty spaces in front of the brightly lit building. "I'm here."

"ETA two minutes," he answered.

"Boy, that was a fast ten," she said with a huff of a laugh.

"No traffic, shots fired, use whatever excuse you want," he informed her. "Almost there."

Chapter Fourteen

Michelle stared over the rim of her coffee mug as he soused the short stack of pancakes he'd ordered with a steady stream of maple syrup. He met her gaze and tipped the syrup dispenser back to slow the flow. "What?"

She shook her head, her gaze dropping to his plate. "You're going to eat all those? In the middle of the night?"

"I think better on a full stomach," he said, brushing her concern aside with a wave of the sticky dispenser before he planted it on the table once more. "It's not like that infusion of caffeine is going to work wonders with your REM sleep."

"True." She set the heavy ceramic mug down with a thud and reached for the sweating glass of ice water the lone waitress had provided when they sat down.

"You're thinking Kayla, huh?" Rather than waiting for her answer, he set to work cutting the stack into bite-size pieces with the side of his fork. "Why would she?" he asked as he speared his first forkful.

"I keep coming back to who knew, and it was you and Kayla," she repeated. "Was it you?"

"Nope," he answered as he chewed. He paused long

enough to gulp down the mouthful, then took a sip of his own water. "But riddle me this—if it was Kayla, why would she, presumedly, hire some man to break into a building she owns in the middle of the night only to steal something no one expected to be there?"

"She knew I would have my laptop with me," she argued.

"Right, but you would be there, too. If the person was there to get you, why didn't they look for you? Why would he take the laptop and bolt?"

"Well, it doesn't make any more sense for my contact at the agency to have arranged it. They already had all the files backed up to the secure off-site server."

"So maybe we're looking at this the wrong way. Maybe it wasn't you or your laptop they were looking for," he said, stabbing up another fork load of pancakes. "Maybe it was the information itself."

"Presuming someone knew I'd be there to access the data."

He chewed as he nodded. "Let me ask you this," he began as he set about attacking his plate again. "If not for the timing and our assumedly closed circle of knowledge, would you suspect Kayla?"

"No."

He looked up and found Michelle appeared to be as surprised by her ready answer as he was. "Gut check complete."

"Yeah, I guess so," she said in a bewildered murmur.

"What do you think she'd say if we showed up on her doorstep in the middle of the night demanding answers?" he asked.

She picked up her discarded coffee cup and cradled it between her palms as if needing to absorb its warmth.

"I don't know." She worried her bottom lip for a moment. "Why? Do you think we should?"

He shrugged, then shoveled another forkful into his mouth. The wheels were turning in her head and he knew his impromptu breakfast might be drawing to an end. She was not going to rest until she had the answers she wanted, and he had the sense she might be ready to roll at any moment.

"You saw the footage from the last time she stayed at the lake house," she said quietly.

He looked up, raising a questioning eyebrow as he chewed. "You think she might be drunk?"

"I have a feeling she wanted out of the hotel for a reason. A little more freedom, a lot more privacy."

Swallowing hard, he reached for his water again. "I wondered if that weekend was a one-off."

"I can't say for certain, but I get the feeling it's getting to be more and more of a problem," Michelle said bluntly. "Pure speculation on my part."

Ethan looked down at his half-demolished plate of pancakes, bid them a silent farewell, then dropped his fork onto the syrup-soaked plate. "Okay, enough speculation," he announced, wiping his sticky hand on a flimsy paper napkin before reaching for his phone.

"What are you doing?" she asked as he thumbed through the screens. "It's nearly 2:30 a.m."

"No time like the present," he insisted, then pressed the phone to his ear. "Yes, hi. It's Ethan Scott," he said when the person on the other end answered. "I'm here with Michelle. There have been some developments." He paused, then looked up, meeting her wide-eyed glare directly as he answered the next question. "No, she's fine." He shifted onto his hip and pulled his wallet from the back pocket of his jeans. Extracting a crisp twenty, he waved it at their waitress, who was busy holding up the other end of the counter. "I'm calling to let you know we're heading out there. Can you send the address?" He listened for a moment, then nodded. "Great. Perfect. See you shortly."

He ended the call, thanked the woman who'd served them and slid from the booth.

"You called her," Michelle asked, scrambling to gather her things and slide from the booth.

"Yep. She sounded fine. Wide awake, too. She said she'd drop a GPS pin in a text." He gestured for her to go ahead of him. "I think we should go separately, and approach using different routes."

"How cloak-and-dagger," she commented as she pushed the diner door open.

"Says the undercover agent to the plainclothes cop," he quipped.

Her smile was slow to blossom, but when she turned back to face him, it landed like a punch to the gut. Her blue eyes twinkled in the bright fluorescent lights streaming out into the night. He was already regretting his suggestion to ride in separate vehicles. After what had gone down in the PP&W offices, he was reluctant to let her out of his sight.

But the situation called for evasive maneuvers, and he wasn't entirely certain he could handle an hour alone in the car with her in the velvety darkness of the early morning hours.

"I'm going to call you," he said, but it came out much deeper and raspier than intended.

"Okay."

"We'll be in communication the whole time, but I'm

going to head north out of town on Highway 72. You take 62 directly there. I should end up only a few minutes behind you."

"And the point of this exercise is…"

"To see if either of us is followed," he finished succinctly.

"You're not the most reassuring guy in the world," she told him, her mouth kicking up into a twisted smile.

"You don't need my reassurance—you're a Fed."

"True."

"You've got this."

Michelle pressed a hand to her chest, rubbing her sternum as if needing to ease an ache there. He was about to offer a change in plan when she let her hand drop to her side and bobbed a quick nod. "Yeah, okay. Let's do this."

IF THERE WAS one thing he learned, it was that Michelle Fraser had abysmal taste in music. Okay, maybe abysmal was a bit harsh, but definitely pedestrian. He'd been able to handle about twenty minutes of whatever pop/soft rock mix she had playing in the background before he had to speak up.

"Are you listening to a playlist or a station?"

"Huh?"

He chuckled. She'd clearly been lost in thought as she drove. Probably not a good thing on a dark and twisting rural highway in the dead of night, though. "Wake up, counselor," he ordered.

"I'm awake, Lieutenant," she retorted.

"If you're awake, I have to assume the music you're subjecting me to is a choice," he said gravely.

"I can turn it off."

The music cut out and he grinned into the night. "Thank you."

"I usually don't pay much attention to the radio. I mostly listen to audiobooks in my car."

"Anything good lately?"

"So many," she answered easily. "Have you read the latest Peterman?"

Ethan grunted. "You listen to legal thrillers? Don't you ever take a day off?"

There was a pause, then she laughed. "Most of the time I listen to either romance or non-fiction, but I figured you didn't and I was trying to make conversation."

"You make assumptions," he said, feigning injury. "I'll have you know I often swap books with my mother and sisters, and I happen to be a big fan of stories with a happily-ever-after."

"Do you believe in them?"

"Happy endings?" he asked, trying not to be offended by the surprise he picked up in her tone. "Sure."

"A lot of people in our line of work get jaded."

"Which line of work are you referring to, policing or lawyering?" he asked, unable to repress his teasing smile.

"Either. Both," she answered with another soft laugh.

He wanted to keep going like this. He wanted to know more about her. "Both can be hard on relationships, but I figure when you find the right person it all works out."

"And have you?" she asked.

"Is this your coy way of asking if I'm involved with someone?"

"I didn't think I was being coy," she countered.

"Right. You weren't. And no, I haven't met the right

person yet." They lapsed into silence, and afraid she wasn't going to reciprocate, he rushed in. "How about you?"

"Me?"

"Relationship?"

"Oh. No." She paused and he could almost hear her frown through the phone. "I've been undercover for two years, so no."

"And your family? Who feeds your to-be-read pile?"

"Mainly newsletters and book reviewers," she replied. "Both my parents were career army. They split when I was young, so I got shuffled around even more than the usual military kid. My mom has retired and lives in Maryland. My dad was killed in action when I was eighteen."

He winced as if absorbing the blow for her. "I am sorry," he said quietly.

"Thank you."

Another silence settled. The hypnotic hum of tires on asphalt nearly lured him in, but then he caught sight of a sign indicating a sharp right turn and forced himself to sit up straighter. "Where are you?" he asked.

"Um, at the corner of dark and desolate," she answered. "GPS says I'm fifteen minutes away, and I turn off the highway in a few miles." A beat passed. "Where are you?"

"Not far behind. I'm showing nineteen minutes and about ten miles from the turnoff."

"You're moving at a good clip," she commented.

"I grew up driving roads like this," he reminded her.

"I grew up in places with streetlights."

"I bet moving to Bentonville was a nice dose of culture shock."

"Some, but not as bad as you'd think. I like seeing stars at night."

He chuckled. "If you think you see stars in town, make sure you look up when you get to the Powers place."

"I should call Kayla and give her at least some heads-up. I need to make sure we can get past the gate. I'm assuming she has locked herself in."

Ethan frowned, not enthusiastic about ending the connection. "We could conference her in," he suggested.

She gave a soft, rueful laugh. "I'm afraid I can't, Lieutenant. She's still my client, and rules of confidentiality apply."

"I wasn't trying to—"

"I know," she said, not letting him finish his thought. "But we're almost there, and I'm a trained federal agent, in case you've forgotten."

"So you say. I never did see any ID," he answered gravely.

"I'll show you my credentials when we get to the house."

"That's what they all say—"

"I'm signing off, Ethan," she interrupted. "Thank you for keeping me company, and for helping me calm down. I'm fine now. I promise."

"Maybe wait until you turn off the highway," he suggested, loathe to end the call.

"I'm signaling for the turn now. Oh, and there are a couple of fairly sharp switchbacks before you get to it, so take it easy."

"You signaled for a turn on an empty highway?"

"I'm a law-abiding citizen. Besides, there's some guy

who drives like a maniac following me, and I'm afraid I'll be rear-ended."

The moment she spoke the words, he spotted a set of headlights striping the highway ahead of him. Letting off the gas, he cringed as a beat-up old farm truck with no working taillights pulled onto the highway ahead of him.

He groaned his annoyance. "No need to worry about me following you now. You have Farmer Fred and his rusty old Ford running interference for you."

"There's someone out this early?"

"There are lots of people who start their days before dawn. Particularly people who run farms or ranches," he replied.

"I suppose that makes sense."

Propping his elbow on the door, he dropped his head into the cradle of his palm as he slowed to a snail's pace behind the rattling pickup. "Hopefully, he's moving from field to field. If not, I'll pass at the first chance I get."

"Don't rush. I'm hanging up now to call Kayla. I'll see you shortly."

Three beeps signaled the end of the call. With a put-upon sigh, Ethan eased off the gas even more to give the farmer some extra room.

He coasted along for a moment, not wanting to press the driver of the truck. The poor guy was probably sipping coffee from a container and trying to ease his way into the day. Ethan felt his own eyelids growing heavier with each passing second. Finally, impatience won out. He rubbed his temple and glared at the reflection of his own headlights in the dented chrome bumper of the truck ahead of him. "Seriously, guy? This is going to be your top speed?"

As if the driver heard him complaining, the truck slowed even more. Ethan tapped his own brakes and lifted his hand to check the speedometer. They were creeping along at less than thirty-five miles per hour on a highway marked for fifty-five.

"Okay, come on. Now you're messing with me," he grumbled.

The safety ridges cut into the pavement at the center line growled their warning as he swung into the other lane to check to see if it was safe to pass. Unfortunately, a bright yellow road sign indicated a sharp turn to the left, precluding any possibility of a safe pass on the dark country road.

"I guess she wasn't lying about those switchbacks," he mumbled as he dropped back into line behind the truck.

The driver ahead slowed even more.

Ethan hit his brakes again, making sure to leave a safe distance between his vehicle and the tailgate of the pickup truck. Part of him wished he was still a trooper on patrol. This guy deserved a ticket for the lack of operating taillights, if not the dangerously low rate of speed. The tree line thickened around them, and the inky darkness of the mountain night seemed to close in.

The road sloped downward as they headed into the lowlands where the Army Corps of Engineers had stemmed the flow of the White River enough to create the lakes that transformed Northwest Arkansas into a sportsman's paradise and a tourist playground.

Coasting down the incline, he tapped his brakes occasionally to slow his momentum. When they rounded the curve and the hill bottomed out. Ethan was about to check if there was enough of a straightaway to punch it past the truck when the other driver signaled a right turn.

Ethan expelled a gust of frustrated breath and hung back, figuring he could be patient a few more minutes. "At least your signals work," he muttered, frowning at the truck's dented tailgate. He craned his neck to scan the right side of the road, hoping to gauge how long he had to wait until the slowpoke turned off. A flash of bright lights coming from his left startled him. Ethan looked into his rearview mirror in time to see a vehicle taking the curve at a high rate of speed and bearing down on him.

Slapping at the dashboard, he activated the emergency flashers, hoping to warn the driver behind him of pickup truck's snail-like pace. But to his consternation, the headlights in his mirror only grew larger. It was another truck. This one larger, with a boxy cab and a wide flat windshield.

"What the—" He trailed off as he tapped his brakes repeatedly, then laid his palm on the horn, giving one long, loud blare in hopes of startling the driver of the pickup truck into getting a move on.

But contrary to the flashing right turn signal, the truck ahead of him swung into the left lane as if it were preparing to pass another car. All too aware of the vehicle on his rear bumper, Ethan pressed the gas pedal to the floor in hopes of shooting ahead of the ancient pickup and creating enough room for the impatient driver behind him to pass.

"It's too early for this," he growled, turning his head in hopes of getting a good glare in at the farmer as he passed.

But to his surprise, the rattletrap old pickup chose this moment to lurch forward. He stayed apace with Ethan's rear quarter panel despite their ever-increasing speed.

And the truck behind him showed no inclination to slow his roll.

Another bright yellow road sign indicated a sharp turn to the right and advised a much slower rate of speed. His hands gripping the wheel, Ethan tapped his brakes in a last-ditch effort to get the truck behind him to slow before they got to the turn.

No luck.

The pickup truck started to drift back over into his lane and he floored the accelerator to get away.

"What the—" He jerked the wheel hard, skidding through the turn with his eyes partially closed. His tires squealed on asphalt. A spray of gravel shot out from under his rear tire when he caught the narrow shoulder of the road. If he made it through this stretch of road in one piece it would be through sheer luck.

Fate seemed to be on his side.

The road straightened after the turn. He spotted a wide shoulder running along some river bottom pastureland and fixed his gaze on it.

He gritted his teeth as the SUV bumped and crunched across the gravel shoulder and then slowed when he hit the softer ground under the overgrown grass along the side of the road. His vehicle jerked to a halt on a rut.

He looked up to see the bigger truck zoom past. Caught in the beams of his headlights, he could see now it was an old hay truck with a bed made of warped plywood. TDP, LCC was painted in script on the passenger door.

His breath came in short staccato bursts as he watched

the truck's taillights disappear beyond the next rise. Twisting in his seat, he tried to catch sight of the pickup, but the door pillar blocked his view. He ducked his head to peer into the side mirror and saw the truck had stopped about a quarter mile back. Ethan rolled his window down and stuck his head out in time to see the driver complete a three-point turn and take off in the direction they'd come from.

Dropping back into his seat, he huffed out a rush of air as he stared at the taillights on the hay wagon. Dimly he registered an insistent female voice ordering him to return to the route. He glanced at the map display. The navigation system was imploring him to get back on the road. He blinked when the order to proceed to the route came through the speakers again. "Did you see what happened here? Give a guy a break."

Ethan drew a shaky breath and then let it seep from his lips. Forcing his shoulders down, he rolled them a couple times. "I was on the route," he complained to the disembodied voice. "Apparently, some people didn't want me to be on the route."

The moment the words slipped out, suspicion set in. On a surge of fear-fueled anger, he punched the gas and fishtailed as he steered the SUV back onto the pavement. Jabbing his thumb at the call button on the steering wheel, he ordered the voice assistant to dial Michelle Fraser's number.

She answered on the first ring. "Hello? Are you lost?"

"Not lost, but delayed," he said, checking his rearview mirror repeatedly.

"Did you stop at an all-night pancake house?"

"I did not." He bit his lip as he settled back into the drive. "Did you make it okay?"

"I'm in. Kayla is awake. I'm putting on a pot of coffee. How long till you're here?"

"Um—" He cut his gaze to the GPS. "I'm still eleven minutes out," he reported.

"You took the scenic tour?" she persisted.

"I'll explain when I get there."

His tone must have told her he wasn't in the frame of mind to joke about it because she sobered instantly. "Is everything okay?"

"I don't know," he confessed. "I don't think so."

"Are you okay?" she asked without missing a beat.

He pressed the accelerator, eating up pavement as fast as he dared to go on the narrow unlit highway. But no matter how his speedometer climbed, he never caught sight of the hay truck's lights.

The GPS interrupted his thoughts to warn him about the upcoming turn onto the road leading to the Powers family lake house. "I'll be there shortly. Are the gates open?"

"Yeah, I left them open for you."

His palms began to sweat where he gripped the steering wheel. "Close them."

"You'll be here in less than ten minutes," she argued. "There's a deputy parked out there."

"I'll call you when I'm at the gate itself. And keep the doors locked."

"Ethan, what's going on?"

"I'm not sure yet, but whatever it is, I don't like it."

"I don't like the sound of this."

"Are you closing the gates?"

"Heading back there now."

"Do not open the door for anyone other than me."

"I won't." He heard Kayla ask what was happening. "We need to close the gates. How do I close the gates?"

He heard Kayla question why and he slammed the heel of his hand against the steering wheel. "Forget the gates. Call the deputy and tell him not to let anybody but me in. Set the alarm. Stay away from the windows."

"Uh, okay," Michelle answered, sounding breathless. "We need to set the alarm."

"I armed it after you came in," Kayla replied.

"The alarm is armed," Michelle reported back to him.

"Good. Hang tight," he said, his voice taut as he turned onto the lake road.

"Talk to me."

"I had a thing with a couple of locals."

"Locals? What kind of thing?"

"I assume they were local. Who knows?"

"You aren't making any sense. Local whats?"

"Farmers, I guess? Cattle ranchers? I don't know." He exhaled his impatience and tried to marshal his thoughts. "I had a couple of trucks tag team me right after we hung up."

"Tag team you?"

"A pickup and a hay hauler."

"At this time of morning?"

"Yeah, well, I guess they start work early around here."

"But there aren't any farms around here. It's nothing but forest for miles," she argued.

"Maybe in the area immediately surrounding the lake, but I got up close and personal with a strip of pasture back there."

"What?" Michelle's voice rose with agitation. Then

she must have pulled the phone away from her face because her voice was more distant when she asked, "Are there any farms around here?"

Kayla was nearby because he heard her answer, "There are some by the highway, but everything on this side is private land. Timber, mostly."

"I was still on the highway when I met up with them, but I don't think they were heading out to tend the fields."

"What are you saying?"

"I'm saying I think someone tried to run me off the road."

Chapter Fifteen

Michelle waited until they had mugs of coffee in hand and taken seats on the tall stools at the marble-topped island in the kitchen before diving in. Taking turns, she and Ethan told Kayla the story of what happened at PP&W and the decision to come to her. When Michelle got to the part where she ended the call with Ethan, she turned to look directly at him.

"Tell us what happened."

"Well, a pickup truck pulled out in front of me on the highway," he began, using the tips of his fingers to turn the mug in a slow circle. "He was going slow and I was getting pretty annoyed, but we were getting close to the switchbacks, so I couldn't pass."

"I know the stretch," she said encouragingly.

"When we reached the bottom of the hill, he had a friend join him."

"A friend?"

"Some jerk driving a truck, you know, the kind used to haul hay?" When they nodded, he tapped the rim of his mug, clearly agitated. "He came out of nowhere, barreling down on me."

"And you have reason to believe they were working together?"

"No proof, only a hunch."

"I thought you were supposed to deal in proof," Kayla said, her tone challenging. "You seem to be big on suppositions these days."

The look Ethan shot her might have frozen a lesser woman in her tracks, but Michelle was discovering Kayla Powers was no one's pushover.

"What's giving you this hunch?" she asked, hoping to keep the conversation on track.

"They seemed to be tag teaming me. The pickup truck slowed down and blocked the passing lane while the truck behind me appeared to be intent on running me over or off the road." He paused for a moment and lifted his mug and took a sip of the coffee. "I guess he succeeded at the last one."

"A strange place to do it," Kayla mused. "If you want to terrorize someone on the roads around here, wouldn't it make more sense to do it up in the hills than down in the river bottom?"

"I think it was more a crime of opportunity," he said dryly. "I don't suppose you know any of the people who own the farms or ranches around here?"

Kayla sat back on her stool and eyed him coolly. "Actually, I do."

"Can you give me a name?" he countered.

"Powers."

The name landed in the center of the room, its final consonant reverberating like the concussion of a bomb.

Michelle waded in, her scalp prickling a warning to choose her words carefully. "The Powers family owns farmland?"

"Ranchland," Kayla corrected. "And yes. It's my understanding they have for years."

"The door of the hay truck was stenciled with TDP, LLC," Ethan informed them, his jaw tight.

"Tyrone Delray Powers," Kayla said, enunciating each name with deliberate care. "Ty's father bought the land."

"So, the people driving those trucks work for you," he said, his level gaze fixed on her.

"Technically, I suppose so," Kayla answered, her stare every bit as direct.

Ethan shifted forward, his posture confrontational. "You have to understand, when suppositions pile this high it looks bad."

"It looks exceptionally bad," she replied.

Kayla's agreement seemed to throw Ethan off-balance.

"I believe it's meant to look bad." She held Ethan's gaze.

"Okay, we get it," Michelle interrupted. "But I have to say I agree with Kayla here. You have a whole pile of circumstantial evidence pointing to Kayla."

"It's getting to be more than a pile," Ethan retorted.

"And you have to admit it's slightly too convenient. All these flashing neon signs keep popping up and point at Kayla saying, 'The Widow did it!' Feels a little too easy, doesn't it?"

"Nothing about this is easy," Ethan muttered. But he leaned back, letting the stool support his weight as he rubbed an exhausted hand over his face.

"No, it's not," Kayla agreed.

"Right. We're all trying to find answers," Michelle insisted.

"I'm not entirely convinced we're all on the same side," Ethan said gruffly.

"I did not try to run you off the road," Kayla asserted, her voice crisp and tart.

"I never said you did," Ethan answered, his tone deceptively calm. "Still, it's awfully convenient people driving vehicles belonging to a ranch you own were involved in the incident."

"It's anything but convenient, and I can prove I was here the entire time," she shot back.

"Yes, having such a robust security system is proving to be the most convenient part of all, isn't it?"

"Enough." Michelle slammed the flat of her palm on the veined marble island as she slid off the stool to stand. When they both turned to look at her, startled by the outburst, she took the time to nail each of them with a hard stare. "We get it. You both have reason to be wary of each other, but bickering isn't going to get us one step closer to figuring out who killed Tyrone and Trey, nor is it going to help me figure out what kind of mess PP&W is in."

When neither of them spoke, she pressed on. "We all have a vested interest in getting to the bottom of this. I believe in working together—the three of us can cover a lot of ground. Can we set the bickering and suspicion aside for now and try to focus?"

Kayla broke first. "What do you need me to do?"

"Tell me who else knew I'd be at the office tonight."

Kayla raised her hands. "I didn't tell anyone."

"Me either," Ethan was quick to add. But then he frowned. "But speaking of security systems...does the one for the office have cameras?"

Frowning, Kayla shrugged. "He got notifications on his phone whenever someone keyed in." Her forehead creased and she closed her eyes as if trying to recall something. "There have to be cameras because he could see on his phone who'd disarmed the alarm. I remember him commenting on what a suck-up Trey's friend Chet was, putting in extra hours at all hours. He said he was going to talk to Hal about it."

"And it's possible Harold Dennis would also have access?"

Kayla sat up straighter. "I'm not sure. Probably. Maybe Benny in IT, too?"

"Ooh. Good thinking," Michelle enthused. "Let's assume someone else does. It would explain how someone knew I was there."

"But it doesn't explain why they took your laptop and left," Ethan interjected.

"No, it doesn't." She turned to Kayla. "I need to explain to you how I came to be here." She cast a sidelong glance at Ethan and drew a deep breath. "A few years ago, an interested party noticed an abnormality in some legal documents," she began, choosing her words carefully.

"Can we have it straight?" Kayla asked, rubbing her forehead. "I'm too tired for legalese. I think if we're going to get anywhere we need to speak plainly."

"I agree," Ethan said with a nod.

"Okay. Someone noticed their name was used as the principal owner of a real estate development company they'd never heard of. When they looked into it, they found it was a shell corporation set up by one of the attorneys at PP&W."

"Which attorney?" Kayla demanded.

"William Powers."

There was a moment of absolute silence as they digested the information.

"But Bill hasn't been active at the firm since he announced his candidacy years ago," Kayla pointed out.

"Yes, I know. But William Powers signed the incorporation paperwork for this company using Judge Walton's name years ago. We assume DevCo was then set up as a client, and money from an influx of real estate transactions started to flow through the firm. As a name partner in the firm, Judge Walton retains financial oversight rights. The financial end of it is pretty murky, but the upshot is, he believed the bulk of the money has found its way into the senator's political action committee and didn't want his name associated with any shady dealings. The uptick in activity combined with the transfers made into the Powers for the People fundraising account raised a red flag for the person who brought it to the complaint."

Kayla wet her lips. "Do you think Bill suspected Ty was on to him?"

"I have no idea." Michelle met Kayla's eyes directly. "But I think I oversimplified things. The way things were set up, I think this was meant to be a long game, and it involved more than your husband and his brother."

"How do you mean?"

"The company was originally registered in the name of Anthony Walton."

"Judge Walton?" Kayla said, clearly shocked by the news.

"Yes. He came across the original articles of incorporation and did a little digging around on his own. He's not entirely convinced William Powers actually filed that paperwork."

"Oh, boy," Ethan murmured.

"In the beginning, they were smart about covering

their tracks, but once William Powers won his first race, things became even more convoluted, and greater sums of money started moving through the shell company. Judge Walton brought the initial transactions to the attention of the Federal Election Commission, who reached out to the Bureau, and here I am."

"What are you hoping to find in the documents you downloaded this evening?" Ethan asked.

"I hope to find a clear-cut paper trail, but hope and expectation are two different things."

"What do you expect to find?"

"I think we're looking at a fairly sophisticated real estate Ponzi scheme. I'm not sure if Senator Powers is the one at the top of this pyramid, or if someone was using his name."

"Either way, I expect to find he's had some low-level associate handling most of the transactions," Kayla hazarded.

"I agree," Michelle said with a nod. "If he is involved, he'd want to be as far removed from the pipeline as possible."

"But Ty..." Kayla frowned. "Do you think this might be why Ty was so wary of Harold Dennis?"

Michelle shook her head. "It's possible. So far, I haven't been able to find any direct interaction between Tyrone and the company in question. The only thing that feels off to me is the senator hasn't done anything to distance himself from the company we're investigating."

"I'm almost afraid to ask," Ethan said, raising both eyebrows.

"DevCo," Kayla whispered.

Michelle nodded a confirmation, turning her attention to Ethan. "What did you find out about the flight plans for the private jet?"

"As far as we can tell, the jet left Northwest Arkansas Regional, made a stop at Reagan National in DC, then flew on to Barbados as stated. It returned to the private hangar at NWA Monday morning."

"Any luck getting a passenger manifest?"

Ethan shook his head. "Stonewalled."

"Most likely because the person you're asking is the person who desperately wants to hide the information."

"But we know Bill went on to Europe," Kayla interrupted, "but Harold…"

Michelle inclined her head. "Yes, Harold. Mr. Dennis managed to fly into and off the island without seeing anyone. He supposedly had to wait to fly back commercial." She cast a sidelong glance at Ethan. "I don't suppose you were able to find him on any commercial flight manifests?"

"The request for information is still out there." He drew a deep breath, then blew it out. "But the airlines and the FAA aren't always quick to share such information. I had to go through Homeland Security to even submit the request."

"And Bill sits on the Senate Homeland Security Committee."

"A convenient coincidence," Michelle drawled.

"Where does that leave us right now?" Kayla asked, her voice husky with fatigue.

"It leaves me in need of a computer and a couple of hours to poke around and see if I managed to swipe anything useful while I was in the office."

"You can use the computer in Ty's office. It's a desktop, but he has full access to the PP&W server."

"I'd rather not use one so connected to PP&W if I can help it," Michelle interjected with an apologetic wince. "Logging on from Ty's might leave a great big footprint."

"I have an ancient laptop around here somewhere," Kayla said, gesturing vaguely. "I'll have to find it and the cord. I mostly use my phone for everything these days."

"If you would look for it, I'd appreciate it," Michelle said firmly. "I'll use Tyrone's desktop if we have no other option, but I'd prefer to have something not connected to the firm's network in any way."

Kayla stood up. "I think it might be in one of the closets upstairs. I'll see what I can find."

The moment she left the room, Ethan turned to look directly at her. "It might be best to use Tyrone's computer after all. What if it isn't someone at PP&W? What if you access the data from the cloud, and it's somebody within your agency?"

"Let's see what Kayla can come up with before we go there, but you don't need to worry about my data."

"I don't?"

"Nope." She reached into the front of her shirt and extracted the thumb drive from the band of her bra. Holding it up triumphantly, she beamed at him. "I always make sure I have backup."

ETHAN AND KAYLA dozed in chairs on opposite sides of Tyrone Powers's spacious home office. She couldn't blame them for sleeping. There wasn't much for them to do other than sit and watch her scan through column after column of data, looking for patterns.

As usual, she let her mind drift as she worked, musing over the absurdity of building such a sumptuous office into a vacation home, but she figured the rich got to be rich because they never stopped working at it. Kayla did say they often entertained clients at the lake house, so Michelle supposed it made sense for Tyrone to have a place to talk turkey while the rest of the world worked hard at having fun.

Ethan jerked upright on a soft snore, and she smiled at the screen as he mumbled an apology, shifted in the tufted leather club chair and drifted off again.

The laptop Kayla had unearthed from a closet was a PC. It appeared to be a few years old, but barely used. She'd plugged her thumb drive into the port and said a prayer to the tech gods she'd grabbed everything she needed.

She worked steadily for a couple of hours, oblivious to her own lack of sleep. Adrenaline coursed through her veins. The answer was close. So close she could almost reach out and grab it. She only needed to let her mind take her to it.

Leaning back in Tyrone's huge leather chair, she curled her knuckles against the bridge of her nose, closing her eyes as she smoothed the arc of her brows. "Relax. You've got this," she whispered to herself.

Embarrassed she'd spoken the words out loud, she sat up and opened her eyes, checking to see if either of her companions heard her little pep talk. But the only sounds in the room were the occasional whir of the laptop fan, Kayla's soft breathing and Ethan's occasional grunts and snorts.

As quietly as she could, she rose, grabbing her coffee mug from the coaster on the desk. She padded into the kitchen, checking the night sky beyond the wall of windows at the back of the lake house. She had an hour, maybe a bit more before the sun started to rise. They'd have to leave within two hours to make it back to Bentonville in time for Trey Powers's memorial service. Time was of the essence, but Michelle was loath to leave before she found the key to the data.

With a fresh mug of coffee, she tiptoed back into the office and resumed her seat. Neither Ethan nor Kayla twitched an eyelid. A part of her envied them their ability to catch a nap at this time. Even if she wanted to, she was too keyed up.

Too close.

She took a sip of the strong black coffee and placed the mug carefully back on the coaster. The soft clink of ceramic on the stoneware coaster was as loud as a starter pistol in her mind. The sound brought her back to the sharp crack of the gunshot and the glass sidelight.

Shaking her head, she shelved all thoughts of what had happened in the PP&W offices for later. Right now, the night was slipping away from her.

Covering her eyes with the palms of her hands, she took three deep breaths before allowing herself to look at the computer screen again. The brief respite did the trick.

The moment she opened her eyes it became clear—the same sequence of five numbers leaped out at her over and over.

It was the employee ID number the server logged each time a specific person accessed a file.

Most associates at PP&W—heck, most employees around the world—failed to realize their every keystroke could be monitored. When Michelle began to fully comprehend what she was seeing, she wanted to kiss Benny in IT square on the lips for his diligence. She also wanted to kick herself. She should have hacked into the firm's human resources files while she was in the server.

With a few taps at the keyboard, she entered a command to isolate only the repetitive employee ID number. With the filter applied, the pattern of moving money into one specific account then immediately out of it into another was so apparent she wanted to weep. She recognized the DevCo client number from the research she'd done on the company. The account receiving the funds was a bank account number familiar to everyone working the case of William Powers's bottomless war chest.

She'd found the pipeline into Powers for the People.

"Bingo," she said softly.

Ethan startled as if she'd shouted. Lifting a hand to rub his eyes, he asked, "You found something?"

"I did," she said, unable to contain the quiver of excitement in her voice. "I found transfers of money into DevCo and the same number out to the Powers for the People contribution account."

"No kidding?" Ethan launched himself from the chair and came around the desk to join her. He braced one hand on the back of the chair and the other on the desk as he leaned in, peering at the monitor. "How do you know these are all DevCo to Powers?" he asked.

"I'll double-check the DevCo number to confirm, but I recognize the numerical sequence. I'm pretty sure it was in the company information I sent to you, if you would double-check for me," she said glancing up at him.

"Hang on." He pulled his phone from his pocket

and began to scroll. A moment later, he read the number out loud.

"That's it," Michelle stated, pointing to the number repeating on the screen. "I have isolated the transactions by this number," she said, indicating the column with the employee ID numbers. "The only problem is I didn't download HR files, so I'm not exactly sure who employee 19544 is."

"There are HR files on Ty's desktop," Kayla said in a groggy voice. Michelle looked over to see the other woman straightening in her chair. "We can log in. If anybody asks, I have every right to look at them, don't I?" she asked, her voice raspy, but firm.

Michelle smiled. "Yes, you do."

She spun in the chair to face the large all-in-one computer built into the credenza behind the desk. Kayla had powered it up earlier, but Michelle had opted for the laptop and thumb drive. She couldn't be certain who knew what, and it was better to do her research with as much stealth as possible.

She shook the mouse, and the screen sprang to life. "Do you know his password?"

Kayla moved to join them. "Yeah. It's 'Kapow.' Capital *K*, lowercase a-p-o-w." When Michelle shot her a look, Kayla blushed. "It was an old joke. Our couple name. You know, like the tabloids?"

Michelle softened as she eyed her...friend? She wasn't exactly sure when she and Kayla had crossed the line from acquaintance to client to friendship, but whatever their relationship was, the trust between them made it something deeper.

She offered a tired smile. "Old jokes are the best jokes. And *Kapow* is a great couple name."

"We thought so," Kayla whispered.

Turning back to the computer, Michelle keyed in the password and the desktop sprang to life. Michelle had fully intended to hack into whatever she needed to get the numbers, but Kayla hadn't exaggerated when she said Tyrone had everything on his computer.

The master dashboard offered up everything she could have ever wanted on a silver platter. If she had come here first, there would have been no need for a late night break-in. She wouldn't have had someone taking shots at her door or stealing her computer. She could have simply asked Kayla for access.

But she'd never been one for the easy route, she thought with a smirk. Plus, it would have meant she had to trust Kayla enough to take her into her confidence, and people in her line of work were wary of giving too much information away.

Sighing, she clicked on the icon labeled Human Resources, and watched as the employee dashboard populated. There, four slots down from the top was the number she'd isolated.

19544.

She followed the line of data across until she saw the corresponding name.

Kayla and Ethan moved in to stand behind her and peered over her shoulder.

"Who is it?" Kayla prompted.

Michelle cleared her throat and shot a glance at Ethan before answering. "It appears our winner is…Harold Dennis."

Chapter Sixteen

After Trey's memorial service, Natalie met mourners at a gathering at the historic Peele Mansion and botanical gardens. She'd invited Kayla and Michelle to avoid gossip, and they'd accepted in order to preserve the illusion of congeniality in the family. With a glass of water in hand, Michelle wandered through the rooms of the old house, marveling at what people once considered fashionable wallpaper and doing her best to pretend she wasn't watching Harold Dennis's every move.

She, Kayla and Ethan had split up, agreeing it wouldn't look good for the three of them to appear overly friendly. Michelle had been grateful for the relative peace of the memorial service. She hadn't slept a wink since her brief nap prior to her visit to the PP&W offices, and fatigue was quickly overtaking her.

Cruising past the brunch buffet laid out in the mansion's dining room, she filled a plate with miniature quiches, some cheese and a selection of bite-size pastries. Protein and sugar would see her through. She certainly didn't need any more caffeine. She'd been jittery all morning.

She was scanning the room when she saw Ethan pull his phone from his belt and accept a phone call. Kayla stood in the small library, making small talk with a few PP&W associates. Michelle noted she'd stayed as far away as possible from the front parlor where Natalie Cantrell held court.

Harold Dennis, Senator Powers and Del all danced attendance on the older woman, pointedly ignoring the presence of Tyrone's widow and heir. Michelle smirked. Those men underestimated Kayla. Had from the beginning. Only Del had the grace to say a few words to her, and he'd broken away as soon as his father caught his eye. Watching the interaction, Michelle couldn't help but think Tyrone Powers had done exactly what he'd needed to do to ensure the future of his firm.

"Ms. Fraser."

Michelle jumped, then flashed a weak smile when she recognized the older man with the commanding baritone. "Judge Walton. How are you?"

The judge shook his head. "Terrible thing. This whole business."

Michelle couldn't help wondering if he knew she was the one sent in to investigate his suspicions. It was possible. After all, someone had to have pulled some strings to be certain she was the candidate Tyrone Powers and Harold Dennis selected to replace Kayla. Still, in all the interactions she'd had with the judge who had been a name partner before ascending to the bench, he'd never given a hint of inside knowledge.

"It is," she concurred, aware she'd taken too long to respond. "I'm sorry, my mind was elsewhere," she said, flashing an apologetic smile. "How are you doing, sir?"

His mouth twitched into a smile. "We've already covered the niceties," he reminded her.

"My apologies," she said, a blush creeping up her

neck. Glancing down at the plate she held, she shook her head. "I think I need to eat."

He nodded. "A good idea. There are some lovely spots in the garden if you need some quiet as well."

She flashed him a grateful smile. "An excellent idea. Thank you, Your Honor."

"Thank you," he replied with a pointed stare. At her puzzled frown, he tipped his head to the side. "For putting up with the family circus. For helping poor Kayla. I know Tyrone would be beside himself at the thought of anyone suspecting her, even for a moment. He trusted her implicitly."

"Oh, well, good," she stammered, thrown by the mere existence of someone who didn't want to throw her client under the bus. "It's been my pleasure to get to know her."

"Not to speak ill of the dead, but I'd wager it has been more pleasurable than dealing with your last client." He sighed. "If Natalie has her way, Trey will be canonized a saint by the end of the week. And they aren't even Catholic."

A burst of laughter escaped her, drawing the attention of some of the others in the room. She averted her gaze when she saw Harold Dennis step out of the parlor, a grave expression creasing his face.

Judge Walton adroitly pivoted so they were facing away from the other man's censorious glare. "I knew Trey from the day he was born, and I loved him, too, in my own way. But I wasn't blind to what he'd become. I know you had an uphill battle ahead of you with him. I also know Matthew Murray and our justice system. Sad to say for Matthew's sake, you likely would have won Trey's battle for him. And I think we both know the victory would have been a testament to your skill rather than his character."

"Yes, sir."

"Go eat," he said with a kindly smile. "You look like you need some respite."

"Thank you, Your Honor," she said, giving him a wan smile as she ducked past him and headed for the doors to the gardens.

She found a wrought iron bench situated in the shade of a hedge and sat down, grateful to be off her feet, though she didn't dare kick off her black pumps. Her body and brain were in shut-down mode, and she didn't know if she could consume enough energy to push through.

Balancing the plate on her lap, she popped a couple of cheese cubes into her mouth and chewed. Her water was almost gone. She should have grabbed a refill before making her escape, but the encounter with the judge had thrown her. Extracting her phone from the small purse she carried, she pulled up Ethan's contact information and typed out a quick text.

I'm hiding in the garden trying to eat. Would you grab me some water? I'm flagging.

"Hello."

Michelle jumped and the plate filled with food slid from her lap to the ground at her feet. She followed its progress, a low moan of frustration seeping from her lips. Then her gaze landed on the polished black wing tips in front of her.

She looked up to find Harold Dennis staring down at her, his stance wide, his arms crossed over his chest and his face lined with disapproval.

"Your client was accessing confidential files from Tyrone's computer," he announced without preamble. "Until a judge rules on the probate, she has no right to those files."

"Until a judge deems a person's most recent will invalid, the executor has every right to access all assets held by the deceased within reason." She tilted her head as she looked up at him. "Did you skim over the part where Tyrone named Kayla Powers executor as well as secondary beneficiary?"

"I don't know what you think you're doing, but—"

Not liking the confrontational tone of his voice, Michelle surreptitiously pressed the call button for Ethan, then slipped the phone into the pocket of her black suit as she rose. "Oh, I think you know exactly what we're doing, Harold," she countered.

Sure she had her feet under her, she lifted her chin to meet his gaze. "Who is the principal owner of DevCo?"

"Excuse me?" His frown deepened. "Why are you asking questions about my client? Don't you have enough on your hands with defending yet another murderer?"

Harold Dennis had never hidden his disdain for the practice of criminal law. When the children and grandchildren of longtime clients found themselves in trouble, he'd been more than happy to pass those cases off to an associate. Taking his discarded casework was how Kayla had carved out her niche within the firm and paved the way for Michelle to step in. She wondered if he realized her presence in his firm was truly a monster of his own creation.

No. Men like Harold Dennis only indulged in the kind of crime that allowed them to keep their hands clean.

Or did they?

Standing toe to toe with the man who thought he called the shots in her career, Michelle decided to go for broke. "Who owns DevCo? And why are you moving money through them to Senator Powers's campaign accounts?"

"I don't know who you think you are—"

"I know who I am," she interrupted. "I'm Special Agent Michelle Fraser working on behalf of the FBI and the Federal Election Commission, and I believe you, Harold Dennis, have been moving money through dummy accounts in order to circumvent campaign finance contribution restrictions. We also think some of that money has been used to finance the senator's personal expenses."

"You're delusional," he said with a scoff.

"I didn't imagine the paper trail you left behind," she responded. "We have all the transactions and they were all done using your PP&W login. You left a digital footprint."

"Somebody must have hacked my computer," he said with a dismissive wave. "Those sorts of things happen all the time. Technology is not as secure as we'd like to believe it is."

"Oh, I know," she said taking a step closer to him. "But I also know the firm's financial data was on a heavily encrypted server, and it took quite a few IT experts to get through the firewalls, but we did it. Benny deserves a raise, by the way."

His jaw tensed and his eyes turned frosty. "You have no proof."

"I have proof like you would not believe," she replied. "Years and years of transactions. We've had a whole team working on this since well before I came here. If you were hacked, Harold, you've been getting hacked for approximately five years."

He laughed, but there was little humor in the sound. "You think you have proof, but you're wrong. Go ahead and file your little report. Whatever data you stole from our company has been…compromised."

Michelle felt a single sinking feeling in her gut. Ethan hadn't been wrong about her contact at the agency. And she hadn't been wrong to make a duplicate copy of those files.

"It seems a lot of things around here have been compromised," she challenged. "Your ethics, your morals and your willingness to get your hands dirty in order to get what you want."

"What is it you think I want?"

"Control of PP&W, for starters," she answered with a shrug. "But we all know you can't have it permanently." She took another small step closer, craning her neck as she gazed up into his angry face. "You'll always have to settle for being the power behind the Powers family, but never the one who actually wields the power. It has to be frustrating."

"You have no idea what you're talking about."

"Is that why you killed them? Tyrone and Trey?" she jabbed her finger into his chest. "You thought you knew what was in Tyrone's will. You thought you would be managing partner for the foreseeable future, possibly for your entire lifetime if you could keep William in office and Del under your thumb."

"I won't listen to this nonsense. You're lucky I don't sue you for slander," he added, pitching his voice low and menacing.

"You're lucky you're not in jail for murder," she shot back as he turned on his heel and started back down the garden path.

Michelle cleared the edge of the hedge and looked to her left. Sure enough, Ethan Scott stood nearby holding a bottle of water. "You catch everything, Lieutenant?" she called out to him, not breaking stride as she followed Harold back to the house.

"Every word," Ethan replied, falling into step beside her.

"I've asked Grace Reed to reach out to the FEC and the FBI. I'll have to figure out who he's got working for them on the inside."

Harold Dennis spun around as he reached the top of the shallow steps leading to the house. "If you don't stop following me, I will file a complaint for harassment. Judge Walton is right inside."

Michelle huffed a laugh. "By all means, let's go in and talk to the judge. Let's ask him who brought me here."

Harold burst through the doors, causing a commotion among the assembled mourners. Michelle trotted to keep up as his long strides ate up the distance between the garden door and the front parlor. Michelle couldn't help noticing his gait didn't match the awkward lope of the assailant who had stolen her laptop.

Harold stopped in the foyer outside the main parlor. He pointed theatrically at the front door. "I'd like you to leave right now," he ordered, his booming voice cutting across the hushed conversations.

Kayla emerged from the small library, as Natalie and the senator rushed from the parlor.

"Harold, for heaven's sake," Natalie said, glancing nervously at their guests.

"What's going on here?" Senator Powers demanded. "Harold, this is hardly an appropriate—"

"Tell her what's appropriate," Harold almost shouted, spittle flying from his mouth as he jabbed one finger in Michelle's direction.

Ethan stepped in. "I believe what would be appropriate at this moment would be to ask you to accompany me down to my office so we could have a little conversation, Mr. Dennis," he said in a congenial tone.

"I'm not going anywhere with you."

"Don't make me arrest you in front of all these people."

Harold sneered. "Arrest me? On what charges?"

"I believe we can start with fraud and campaign finance violations," he said, sliding a glance at Michelle for confirmation. When she nodded, he raised both eyebrows as if challenging the other man to say whether he'd had enough.

But Harold Dennis didn't know when to give in. "You have no evidence," he said, enunciating each word.

"I don't know who you think you have in your pocket, Harold, but I have this."

Michelle reached into her suit pocket and pulled out a thumb drive.

It wasn't the one with the data downloaded from PP&W files. The original was locked in the safe in Ethan's hotel room. But Harold wouldn't know as much. "I made a backup copy of all the files."

Harold's face blanched. Natalie Cantrell and Senator Powers stepped up beside him, but their expressions were clouded with doubt.

"What about campaign finance?" Senator Powers demanded.

"The political action committee Mr. Dennis established for you prior to your first campaign, Powers for the People?"

"Yes," he replied, still looking puzzled.

"Haven't you ever wondered where the bulk of those contributions come from?"

"The same place most contributions come from," the senator answered readily. "Individual citizens, interested businesses, organizations who support the policies I support as a legislator."

"And you've never wondered how there was no ebb and flow in the cash flow coming into your accounts?" Michelle asked.

William Powers shook his head. "I'm not an accountant. I don't audit the books. As for the rest, I assumed Tyrone was keeping the balance on an even keel."

"Tyrone," Harold blurted, his voice thick with derision. "Your brother hardly lifted a finger to ever help you in any of your campaigns."

"That's not true," Natalie and Kayla answered almost in unison.

"And you," he said, turning on Kayla. "You couldn't be content to guzzle your wine and spend his money? You have to make a grab for the firm?"

"I did no such thing," Kayla shot back.

"You had him name you executor of his will and managing partner," Harold cried. "If that isn't cause enough for suspicion, I don't know what is," he said to Ethan.

"It was indeed cause," Ethan assured him. "But, as you mentioned earlier, we haven't found any evidence

Mrs. Powers had means, motive or opportunity. You, on the other hand—"

"I was—"

"Faking a trip to a Caribbean island so you could claim to be out of the country when you made your grab."

"What? How? I flew down there after dropping Bill off in DC," he asserted.

"And flew back the following morning," Ethan countered. "We've spoken to the pilot and attendant who crewed the plane y'all used. It's a sort of private plane timeshare, isn't it? One purchased by the company you established in Anthony Walton's name on behalf of William Powers."

"What?" The senator startled at the mention of his name, but Judge Walton stepped forward, unruffled.

"I am the one who found the articles of incorporation," he said firmly. Fixing his most judicial gaze on the senator, he asked, "Did you file them on behalf of a company called DevCo using my name as principal?"

"What?" William repeated. "No. Of course not."

"They were submitted with your name," Judge Walton calmly responded.

"But they were entered into the PP&W system by Harold Dennis," Michelle interjected smoothly.

"Mr. Dennis, who saw absolutely no one in Barbados before returning to Arkansas on the morning after Tyrone and Trey Powers were found murdered," Ethan added. "The flight attendant said he overheard you arguing with someone on the phone. He said he assumed the person on the other end of the line was a woman because you kept telling the other person whatever they'd found meant nothing." He paused to let the possibility of witness testimony sink in. "But it wasn't a woman, was it? It was Tyrone. Your friend. The man you mentored. He was about to topple your house of cards and you couldn't let it happen."

Harold Dennis's face was nearly purple with rage, his fist clenched tight at his sides, but when he spoke his voice was calm. "Again, where is your proof?"

"I don't have it all together yet," Ethan replied with a casual shrug. "But you know who does?" Wearing a smile Michelle'd swear was filled with pride, he pointed to her. "She does. We'll start with fraud, it's as good a foundation as any." He turned to face her and inclined his head, brows lifted. "Do you want to do the honors, or should I?"

The warmth in her face slid down to her heart, then settled in her belly. She'd been right to press dial when she found herself alone with Harold Dennis. She'd needed backup and Ethan provided it.

Gazing up at him, she realized she was content to be done with it all. "You know what? This is your backyard. You bring him in; we'll work out the rest from there."

"I'll take him," Sheriff Stenton volunteered. When Michelle and Ethan turned to him in unison, he gave them a paternal smile. "You two look beat, and it's going to take a couple hours to get him processed, anyway."

"A couple of hours?" Harold Dennis cried. "It does not—"

"Maybe longer," the sheriff said, talking over the indignant man. "Cuffs, or you coming along peacefully?" he asked Hal.

"You will not cuff me," Hal retorted. "And I want my attorney."

"Oh, sure," Sheriff Stenton answered easily, hooking a big hand through Harold Dennis's elbow. "Which one you want?" he asked, gesturing to the assemblage.

The PP&W associates turned away almost as one—like a school of fish sensing the approach of a predator.

Harold swiveled to shoot a pleading look at William Powers. The senator raised his hands to indicate he couldn't risk touching Harold's predicament. "Hal, what have you done?" he asked as he took Natalie's arm and stepped back.

Harold's jaw set into a thin line, but Michelle caught the sheen of moisture in his eyes as he fixed his gaze on the mansion's front door. "Let's get this farce over with," he said stiffly.

Sheriff Stenton turned back to Michelle and Ethan. "Get some rest. I'll call when he's ready to entertain visitors."

Anxiety twisted her gut as they followed the sheriff and her suspect out into the wide veranda of the old mansion. "I should go with him. I'll need to get someone from the Bureau field offices in either Tulsa or Little Rock, and—"

She didn't realize she'd been twisting her hands together until Ethan placed his hands over them to still her movements. "The sheriff is right. We won't be any good to anyone until we get some rest and clear our minds. Make a call to get someone here, but then shut it down for a moment." He gave her clasped hands a gentle squeeze and her gaze flew to his. "We've gotten this far. We'll sort it all out once we can think straight."

"Right."

Her hands felt cold when he took his away, and she quickly stuffed them into the pockets of her suit jacket. She ran her thumb over the plastic stick drive she'd used to call Dennis's bluff. Ethan had been the one to suggest it. He'd been right. Working together, they made a good team.

Once they'd seen Harold loaded into the back of the sheriff's SUV, Ethan nudged her in the direction of her own vehicle. She turned to look up at him as they stood on the curb. "Have I thanked you yet?"

"Thanked me?"

She shrugged. "You helped nail my investigation, but yours is still—" She let the thought drift away on the breeze.

"Ongoing," he supplied firmly. "But I think you may have helped with it as well."

"You think so?" she asked, tipping her chin up to meet his gaze.

He nodded, then opened the driver's door for her. "I'm hoping I can convince you to work with me on it some more."

"I'm happy to help however I can," she said as she stepped into her vehicle.

"Great. Text me after you've slept some, and I'll meet you down at Stenton's offices. Harold should be good and riled up by the time we get there," he said with a grin.

Michelle couldn't help smiling back. "Just where we want him," she agreed.

He backed up to allow room for her to close the door. "See? I told you. Like recognizes like, Ms. Fraser. I knew you were a cop down to your bones."

She rolled her eyes and reached for the door handle. "Yeah, yeah. You were right, Lieutenant."

"See you in a couple hours," he called as she closed the door.

Michelle drew in a deep breath as she started the car. Ethan raised his hand in a half wave, then started for the side street where he'd parked his vehicle. She watched him go, her stomach still twisting and the quiet of the car's interior filling in all the space around her.

"Right, but will I see you after that?"

Chapter Seventeen

Their reunion at the Benton County Correctional Complex wasn't going as Ethan had anticipated. As a matter of fact, they hadn't been reunited at all. He'd seen several people dressed in standard issue Fed suits come through the offices, but hadn't caught so much as a glimpse of Michelle.

Alas, he'd had more than his fill of Harold Dennis, and his lawyerly non-answers.

Sheriff Stenton must have sensed his growing frustration, because when the dinner hour approached, the older man volunteered Ethan for the food run.

"You're running on empty, son. Get out of here, breathe some air, make whatever call you keep checking your phone for," he added with a teasing smirk. "Old Hal in there isn't going anywhere. The Feds have their hooks in him nice and deep, thanks to Ms. Fraser."

Ethan must have jolted at the mention of her name because Stenton laughed. "Go. Get out." He rocked back on his heels and crossed his arms over his chest. "You might oughta try the Daisy Dairy Bar if you haven't already. Real popular place."

"Is it?"

"Heard your friend Ms. Fraser say she was real partial to their pineapple shakes," the sheriff informed him. "Me, I'm more of an onion ring man." He gave his rounded belly a pat. "But Mrs. Stenton is on one of her health kicks, so it's salad for me."

Ethan eyed the older man through narrowed eyes. "The Daisy Dairy Bar?"

"Mmm-hmm," Stenton hummed, looking off into the middle distance.

Smiling at the man's lack of acting skills, Ethan ducked his head in defeat. "Pineapple milkshakes, huh?"

"That's what I heard."

Checking his phone as he stepped out into the bright sunshine, Ethan growled when he found no texts or calls from Michelle. He hadn't been expecting a big gushing thank you, but he thought after all they'd been through over the course of the week, he'd at least rate a good-bye message.

"Hello."

His head jerked up, and he saw Michelle Fraser leaning against his SUV, and two foam cups sitting on the hood. She'd stripped off her suit jacket. The sleeveless blouse she wore exposed softly curved arms. The tight black skirt clung to her rounded hips and stopped just above her knee. She looked good. Tired, and a little rumpled, but good.

Almost too good.

He had to remember she wasn't likely to stay in these parts now that her case was wrapping.

"Fancy meeting you here," he said, unable to conjure up anything more original.

"I texted Bud and told him you needed a break," she said as she pushed away from the side of the vehicle.

"Oh, you did, now?" He raised both eyebrows. "Bud, is it?"

"We bonded over our love of the Daisy Dairy Bar." She smiled, then reached for one of the cups. "I wasn't sure what flavor you liked best, but I figured I couldn't go wrong with good old vanilla."

He accepted the cup and paper-wrapped straw. "I like most anything, so thank you." He nodded to the cup beside her. "I'm guessing you're having pineapple?"

Her eyes widened and she nodded in grim understanding. "He's giving away my secrets."

"Not all of them," Ethan assured her.

"Only the most important ones," Michelle said as she lifted the cup and placed the straw to her lips. She drew on it greedily, and Ethan's mouth went dry. "I didn't peg the sheriff as the type who'd give away the key to winning a woman's heart so easily."

"Is that the key?" he asked, his voice gruff.

"One of them," she said, color tingeing her cheeks as she ducked her head. "How's it going in there?"

"He had pretty much shut down by the time your team was done with him," Ethan said, unwrapping his own straw and jabbing it into the lid.

"Yeah. Sorry about that," she said with a grimace. "If it makes you feel better, he didn't give up much for us either."

"But you have your evidence," he reminded her.

"We do," she conceded.

"Catch any heat?" He took a sip of his shake, trying to play his question off as casual concern.

"Some," she said with a shrug. "Got a bit of grief about breaking cover, but once I relayed our suspicions about my point of contact, it diverted their attention."

"As it should. So, uh—" he looked away as he mustered the nerve to ask what was really on his mind "—what's next for you?"

"I'm not sure," she said, sipping at her shake again. "I think…" She glanced over at the razor wire-topped fence. "I think I'm ready to live aboveground for a while though, I can tell you that much."

"No more undercover work?"

"No." She bit her bottom lip. "I think I'd like to have a life, you know?"

He nodded. Unable to stand the distance between them any longer, he moved to lean up against the SUV beside her. "I think you've earned it."

They stood side by side for a full minute, neither of them moving or talking.

"Where do you think you'll go?" he asked.

At the same time, she said, "I think I'm going to take some leave."

"Oh, sorry. Go ahead," he said.

"No, uh…" She laughed. "I'm not sure. I think I'll be staying here for a while."

"You are?" he asked, turning toward her.

She smiled and nodded, pivoting in his direction. "Yeah. I mean, I have an apartment here and a job… I think."

"You mean with Kayla?"

"We haven't discussed anything formally, but I figure she's going to need some help," she answered.

"I might need some backup with this nasty double homicide I'm working," he grumbled.

"Wow. I had no idea I'd be so in demand. I'll have to sort out what I'm going to do about the Bureau. Anyone who says juggling multiple jobs is easy is really a clown."

"You're killing me here," he confessed in a grumble.

She looked up, her bright eyes lighting with pleasure and mischief. "Am I?"

"You know you are."

"How am I supposed to know—"

He set the cup on the hood of the car, then snaked an arm around her waist to pull her close. "You know because I know."

"And like recognizes like, Lieutenant?" she asked, tipping her head back, an inviting smile twitching her mouth.

"Yes." He dipped his head, his mouth mere millimeters from hers. "You and me. We're alike."

"Yes, we are," she agreed. Then she lifted up onto her toes and closed the distance between them.

Her mouth was soft and sweet, and the tangy, tropical taste of pineapple clung to his lips even after they broke the kiss. He held on to her, not willing to step out of the bubble they'd created in the midst of murder and mayhem. Needing to stay in the happy place they'd found in each other for just a moment longer.

"One more," he whispered. "It's going to be a long night, and I'm going to need backup if I'm going to make it through."

Michelle smiled as she wound her arms around his neck. "Better make it two. You might need backup for the backup."

"Good thinking," he murmured as he lowered his mouth to hers again. "Very. Good. Thinking," he said, punctuating each part of the compliment with a kiss.

When she pulled back with a sigh, he pressed his

forehead to hers. "I think I'm supposed to go to this dairy bar place and score some illicit onion rings for your friend, Bud. Want to ride along?"

Michelle shook her head as she snagged her cup from the hood of the car. "Can't. We're interviewing the senator next," she informed him. "But here." She reached into her ever-present tote bag and pulled out a grease-stained white bag. "I've got you covered."

* * * * *

#2151 TARGETED IN SILVER CREEK
Silver Creek Lawmen: Second Generation • by Delores Fossen
A horrific shooting left pregnant artist Hanna Kendrick with no memory of Deputy Jesse Ryland...nor the night their newborn son was conceived. But when the gunman escapes prison and places Hannah back in his crosshairs, only Jesse can keep his child and the woman he loves safe.

#2152 DISAPPEARANCE IN DREAD HOLLOW
Lookout Mountain Mysteries • by Debra Webb
A crime spree has rocked Sheriff Tara Norwood's quiet town. Her only lead is a missing couple's young son...and the teacher he trusts. Deke Shepherd vows to aid his ex's investigation and protect the boy. But when life-threatening danger and unresolved romance collide, will the stakes be too high?

#2153 CONARD COUNTY: CODE ADAM
Conard County: The Next Generation • by Rachel Lee
Big city detective Valerie Brighton will risk everything to locate her kidnapped niece. Even partner with lawman Guy Redwing, despite reservations about his small-town detective skills. But with bullets flying and time running out, Guy proves he's the only man capable of saving a child's life...and Valerie's jaded heart.

#2154 THE EVIDENCE NEXT DOOR
Kansas City Crime Lab • by Julie Miller
Wounded warrior Grayson Malone has become the KCPD's most brilliant criminologist. When his neighbor Allie Tate is targeted by a stalker, he doesn't hesitate to help. But soon the threats take a terrorizing, psychological toll. And Grayson must provide answers *and* protection to keep her alive.

#2155 OZARKS WITNESS PROTECTION
Arkansas Special Agents • by Maggie Wells
Targeted by her husband's killer, pregnant widow and heiress Kayla Powers needs a protection plan—pronto. But 24/7 bodyguard duty challenges Special Agent Ryan Hastings's security skills...and professional boundaries. Then Kayla volunteers herself as bait to bring the elusive assassin to justice...

#2156 HUNTING A HOMETOWN KILLER
Shield of Honor • by Shelly Bell
FBI Special Agent Rhys Keller has tracked a serial killer to his small mountain hometown—and Julia Harcourt's front door. Safeguarding his world-renowned ex in close quarters resurrects long buried emotions. But will their unexpected reunion end in the murderer's demise...or theirs?

HICNM0523

HARLEQUIN
PLUS

Try the best multimedia subscription service for romance readers like you!

Read, Watch and Play.

Experience the easiest way to get the romance content you crave.

Start your **FREE TRIAL** at
<u>www.harlequinplus.com/freetrial</u>.